Life in the rugged Wisconsin logging country was no picnic for 12-year-old Jed—or for his parents. Jed grimaced at the thought of his earlier mistakes in helping out as his dad's "hired man"—and how he had lost money for the family. Sure, Dad had forgiven him. But Jed wanted fiercely to make it up to him, and to the others.

There was only one way—kill the great white-tail buck—the Big One—and bring him home for food. Food was as good as money . . . and the family's bills had been mounting daily.

"I can do it," thought Jed, "if only I can get my own rifle . . ."

Winter of the White-Tail Buck

Jeanne Hovde

Illustrated by Carl Hauge

David C. Cook Publishing Co.

ELGIN, ILLINOIS—WESTON, ONTARIO
LA HABRA, CALIFORNIA

David C. Cook Publishing Co., Elgin, IL 60120
Printed in the United States of America
Library of Congress Catalog Number: 75-36698
ISBN: 0-912692-88-X

To My Family

CONTENTS

1

Edge of Danger

JED CRAIG FOLLOWED ALONGSIDE as his father
strode partway up the long steep incline, kicking
through the snow with his heavy leather boots as
he went. Stopping, he pushed his red hat back and
stroked the bulk of black hair covering his wide
forehead.

"Maybe we ought to unload her, Son." Mr.
Craig's dark eyes studied the load of 16-foot red
oak logs sitting at the bottom of the hill. It was a
massive load for the old Ford, only a ton-and-a-half
truck.

"If we unload here," protested Jed, "we'll have to
skid each piece out to the next landing. We'll never
make another load today."

"There's a good five inches of new snow, plus
what we had yesterday, and a pretty slick base. It
pulls hard. I'm not sure it'll hold." Mr. Craig had

9

already made one try, and the truck hadn't climbed the grade.

"We can make it with the tractor hooked on, Dad. I know we can."

For a 12-year-old, Jed already had considerable experience in tractor driving. For that matter, considerable experience in a good deal of men's work. Unlike his father, Jed was of slight build, though as his father always said, "hard as nails." But in coloring and temperament, he favored his father highly.

Jed's father was logging on the family woodland to boost the farm income. It was difficult making a living for a family of six on a small farm in their northern Wisconsin area, and since Jed was the oldest he had to stay out of school for a day now and then to give a hand. The woodland adjoined the family farm, and it raised a good crop of timber even though it was all hills.

"We could go home for the plow and go through the whole trail again," his dad suggested.

"But that means time, Dad."

Getting a load ready was a slow process. As Dad cut and trimmed each log, Jed skidded with Maude and Babe, the two dapple horses, to a cleared landing. There the logs were loaded with the tractor lift. Often Jed had to brush out a new skidway, as his dad harvested only the mature trees. That meant scattered cutting.

"I suppose we can give her one try," agreed his

dad. "It sure would save a whale of a lot of time."
He strode back to the truck and checked the binder
securing the logs. "Bring the tractor from the landing, Jed, and the two heaviest chains."

Jed spun on his heel and hurried up the hill in
the opposite direction to the landing where they
had been working.

To the right side of the truck was a steep drop to
a small lake. Though the house was out of sight at
the far end of the lake where it stood, Jed heard the
door bang, telling him that his mother was doing
her daily chores.

He lifted the heavy chains from the skidway and
boosted them on the tractor. Then he hoisted himself above the drawbar, flung his leg over the seat,
and bounced down into driving position. The tractor started on the first try and lumbered down the
trail under Jed's guidance, heaving from side to
side as it raised itself over the uneven ground of
the trail. Jed swayed with the movement of the
tractor. At the bottom of the hill, he backed the
tractor to the front of the loaded truck.

Mr. Craig unwound the chains and secured one
end of each to the tractor, and the other to the front
of the truck. The tire of the big tractor came up to
his chest as he stood giving directions to Jed. He
spoke above the noise of the motor. "As soon as I
have the truck started, take up the slack in the
chain. Are you in first gear, low range?"

Jed nodded.

"Keep it there unless we gain enough speed so you can put it in high. As soon as we get moving, give it the gun. We're going to need all the speed we can get to make it up that hill. I'll signal a raised hand when I'm ready."

Jed nodded his OK.

His dad gave a final salute of good luck and pulled himself up into the truck.

From Jed's position high on the tractor, the hill looked somewhat steeper than it had when his feet were on the ground. He turned and saw a whiff of smoke from the truck exhaust and his dad's raised hand.

Jed checked his gears, tightened the slack, and began opening the throttle. The heavy tractor dug in momentarily and moved slightly to the left as the two engines started the truck in motion.

Jed opened the throttle wide, leaned back in the seat, and they began climbing the hill slowly. He had hoped to gain more speed. The load was heavier than he had judged, but they were making progress. Halfway up, they started to slow, and as the truck reached the steepest part of the incline, Jed saw the wheels slip, then spin. The tractor hesitated under the weight of the pull. It coughed and jolted. The base was too slick for the truck to take hold, and the tractor could not keep it moving. With one final snort, the motor stopped.

They were slipping backward. Jed set the brakes, perspiration rising beneath his heavy wool clothing. The truck jerked up as his father pulled the emergency brake, and Jed realized instantly that it was only the tractor's weight that held down the front end of the truck. On the steep grade, the long logs overbalanced the truck, nearly swinging the front end off the ground. As Jed braked with every ounce of strength in his body, the truck veered to the right.

Mr. Craig's face was panic-stricken, his knuckles white and taut as he gripped the steering wheel.

Jed could see over the embankment, and the drop became a certainty. They would both be killed, smashed against the trees as they hurled to the lake below. What would become of their family? His younger brother Jared and his mother surely could not do the providing, and Sari, Jed's twin sister, hadn't been well.

He looked again. With teeth set, his father was struggling to steer the truck. They were gaining speed.

In that last terrifying moment, as they neared the bottom of the hill, Jed felt the back right wheel go over the edge. The side of the truck cracked into a huge white oak on the edge of the embankment. The racket thundered through the woods as the tree trembled violently. The truck's front end raised from the ground, and Jed screamed in agony, "Please, God!" as it balanced on the edge.

2

The White-Tail Buck

MR. CRAIG GENTLY OPENED the truck window. "Start the tractor, Jed, and give a slow pull. If we can settle the front end down, we've got a chance."

Although Jed could not speak, he followed instructions. A steady pull brought the front wheels to rest on the ground. Then he locked the brakes.

His dad cautiously descended from the truck, then ran to block the tractor wheels. His chest sank in relief as he wiped his brow with a jacket sleeve. He was covered with perspiration.

"It's all right, Son. You can get down now."

Jed's knees buckled as he grabbed for his father. "I was wrong, Dad. We were nearly killed!" He flung himself into his father's arms.

"It's all right. Just thank God," said his father. He guided Jed to a ledge along the edge of the trail. "We'll rest a few minutes."

Jed laid his head in his hands, and they sat in silence. Right now, being plain old dependable Jed didn't look nearly as bad as it usually did, but he could hardly lay claim to even that.

Finally his dad spoke. "I guess we were both a little reckless." He put one arm around Jed's shoulders and gave a squeeze. "We won't mention this to your mother. It would only upset her."

Jed agreed.

"Feeling better, Son?"

"I feel OK now."

"Then the two of us had better figure a way out of this mess."

By late afternoon, both Jed and his father were exhausted from plain hard toil. With the use of jacks, ropes, and chains, they had managed to unload without losing the truck, although three logs had gone over the embankment, and it was doubtful that they could ever be recovered. They got the truck back on the logging road without serious damage, but they were no further ahead than when they had entered the woods that morning.

"A fellow sure can make a lot of trouble for himself, can't he?"

"That's true, Son, but it's a sure way of learning. There's no use looking back. What's done is done. We forget it and go on from here."

Down the road Jed heard the familiar sound of the school bus grind to a halt at their driveway. Then came the called good-byes of a Friday afternoon, and the spirited scuffling of his brother and sisters as they ran to the house. When it was quiet in the wooded hills, you could hear for miles in the valleys below.

"It's that time already," his father said. "We'd better call it a day."

"I'll second that," Jed agreed. "There's still two hours' work in the barn."

The tractor and truck were left in the woods. Jed climbed on Babe's broad back, and his dad mounted Maude.

Twilight came early and, as Jed neared the edge of the woods, the lighted windows of home beckoned a special welcome to him that December day. Home was humble but warm, a simple white frame house with a natural stone chimney on the front side.

The sound of frying chicken greeted them at the doorway, and Jed breathed deeply to inhale the full aroma of mince pie drifting from the kitchen.

"Here's Daddy and Jed!" yelled Gretchen as she jumped up to greet them. "And there's chicken and pie for supper."

"Hey, now, that's going to be a real treat." Jed gave an affectionate tug at her thick brown pigtails, and the end curls snapped smartly as he released them. "Did you make the pie?"

Gretchen cocked her head to one side and put her hands on her hips. " 'Course not. I can't make pie. I'm only seven."

Jed teased. "Yeah, but you're an awful bright seven."

His mother came to the kitchen doorway. "Wash and come to the table. Supper is ready. How did the day go?"

Jed pretended not to hear.

"Not too bad," Dad answered. He put his arm around Jed's mother and turned her around toward the kitchen. "We had some trouble with the truck that took time. It was a big job, so we never did get to the mill."

"Oh dear, and Jed stayed out of school for a whole day."

"We're in good shape for tomorrow though."

Jared, who had already begun the barn chores, flung the door open and stamped his feet on the entry rug. He was only a year younger than Jed. "I heard Maude whinny, so I knew you were home. Is Dad still at the mill?"

"No," answered Jed. "We never got to the mill. We had some trouble with the truck."

"Everybody to the table," called Jed's dad.

"Come on, Gretchen, I'll race you." Jed held her back by the shirt and stepped out ahead.

"Jed!" Her squeal faked annoyance.

Sari, a small, frail girl who was dark like Jed, came to her defense. "Mom, Jed's teasing Gretchen." At birth, Sari had been the weak twin; and after her first bout with pneumonia when she was only a year old, the illness had occurred often.

18

Jed's mother had cared for her well, and in the last two years she had gained considerable strength, though she still tired easily.

Jed, usually none too happy with her performance, frowned at her. "Why don't you leave us alone and give Mother a hand?"

"Everything's ready." Mother set the milk on the table.

Dad asked the blessing and Jed added a silent request—for special protection in the woods. He was finishing his mince pie when a demanding knock sounded at the back door. Mother answered.

Harold Daager's form filled the doorway. Stepping aside to let his son, Emery, gain entry, he stooped to avoid hitting his head on the top doorjamb, and covered the distance to the table in three steps.

"Evening, Mrs. Craig, John." His voice boomed through the kitchen. "Emery wanted to see Jed. Said he wasn't in school today."

Mr. Craig pushed his chair back. "He stayed home to give me a hand."

Mr. Daager twisted a kitchen chair backward, and burdened it with his huge frame, one leg on either side of the back.

Jed had risen to meet Emery, his closest friend, and they talked quietly near the doorway. Emery was already a good five inches taller than Jed, and only time was needed for him to become a second Harold.

Emery always did exciting things. "There's a skating party tonight at Crex Landing," he said. "Dad will take us down if you can go."

Sari overheard the conversation. "Mom, may I go, too? There's a skating party at Crex Landing."

"Not her," whispered Emery.

Jed looked hopefully toward his dad for an answer. "Could I go?" He ignored Sari's pleading, but prepared to defend himself against it.

"I'm afraid I'll have to say no, Son. We still have work tonight, and a big day ahead of us tomorrow."

Jed was disappointed, but he was tired, too. He shrugged his shoulders toward Emery. "I'd only have to take Sari along, anyway."

Emery turned his back to the table and scowled. "Can't you ever do anything you want to?"

Mr. Daager was still talking. "Well, John," he said, "I guess the Big One outsmarted us again." He spoke of the huge white-tailed buck that had roamed the surrounding area for several years, but always disappeared when the hunting season arrived.

"I didn't get a glimpse of him this year," said Mr. Craig. "But I'm satisfied that the hunting season is over. I've got a lot of work to do around here."

"John got a nice buck," Mother said.

"But we all know what he was after." Harold Daager laughed. " 'Course we all are," he admitted. "But next year Emery will be in the woods too."

Emery, hunting? A pang of envy stabbed through Jed.

Mr. Daager glanced at Emery with admiration. "Those legs of his are strong as oak posts. He can really hold up. Things will be different then."

3

Shake-Up

JED'S DAD RESTED HIS ELBOW on the table and brushed his forelock to the side. "Jed may be hunting with me, too."

Jed was struck with surprise.

Harold Daager sized him up from top to bottom, what there was of him. "That so, now? You think he can take it?"

"He's hard as nails," Dad said, "and dependable. He has a lot of responsibility around here."

Jed could scarcely believe what his father was saying. It nearly erased the sting of Mr. Daager's critical words and insulting stare. He said goodbye to Emery in a daze.

"Did you really mean that, Dad, about my going hunting?"

"I meant it, Jed. When you can handle responsibility, it's time for some privileges. But it will be hard to come by a rifle."

The confidence expressed by his father left Jed eager to complete his duties. He rose early the following morning, did his farm chores, and sat talking with his mother about the Christmas preparations while she made breakfast.

"I'll get a tree today," Jed said. "If I have time while Dad's at the mill, I'm going 'way back to the Christmas tree swamp on the southeast forty."

"That's such a long way. Can't you find something that won't be so hard to get?"

"I want an extra-special tree this year, for Gretchen—a really big one—and for all the relatives coming, too."

Mrs. Craig took the biscuits from the oven. "She's already asking who is going to put the baby Jesus in the crib this year."

"It's Jared's turn."

"He remembers that, and Sari's turn to carry the candle." His mother set the coffee on the table and sat down across from him.

"Shouldn't Sari be up helping?" Jed asked.

"Sari needs a lot of rest. She isn't as strong as the rest of you children."

"Have you set aside the rump roast from Dad's buck?"

"Sari marked 'Christmas Dinner' all over the package in big red letters. There's no chance of it being used ahead of time."

"The uncles and Granddad sure look forward to that venison dinner out here, don't they?"

"It's one of the things they remember from when they were boys. And this was where your grandfather raised his family, so it's always been home to him."

Dad came in for breakfast. "Jared is taking care of the cattle so that Jed and I can get an early start."

"I hope you have a good day," said Mrs. Craig. "We really need to have that check before Christmas."

"Don't worry, Mother," Jed assured her. "There'll be logs at the mill today."

There was a sprinkling of new snow, but the sun was coming up fast in the east, and in the crisp cold air, even Maude and Babe seemed eager to begin the day. They stepped lively as the party headed back to the woods to start the activities which they had abandoned the day before.

"Do you think you'll have any trouble going up empty, Dad?"

"No," said his father. "I'm sure we won't. I'll back up the opposite hill and get a good run for it. After I'm over the crest, you bring the tractor up behind me. Then you can go back and skid."

After the truck climbed the hill in third gear, Jed followed with the tractor. Then he slid back down the road to where the logs lay, thrust the skidding tongs into one end of a log, and whistled to Maude and Babe. Picking up the evener fastened behind them, he snapped the reins lightly.

25

"Back, Maude; back, Babe." Gently he urged them into position. Then he hooked the tongs to the ring on the evener and fastened the reins to Maude's collar. They would follow the trail to the next landing without being driven.

"Go, girls." Jed ran out ahead. He loved to see the horses work. Every muscle seemed to bulge as they laid into the pull, their hot breath steaming from their nostrils. Gaining momentum, their hairy feet whooshed into the glistening snow, flicking it to the side in rhythm at every step. The harness and evener jingled a musical accompaniment. They halted their prance at the landing, pulling up alongside another log.

Dad called, "Bring the chain saw and gas. I'll have to cut another few logs to fill out the load." He motioned to the side. "I think there are a couple of trees up here that we can take."

Jed left the horses at the landing and started after him. When he reached his dad, he was standing at the base of a large red oak, looking up. "Even when you know they're mature," he said, "a man has to think a long time before he makes up his mind to cut a tree like this. It's probably been growing for close to a hundred years." In his dad's eyes was the look of honest reverence.

"I understand, Dad. You have to be sure it's really needed."

"That's right. Things of nature are for our use; but even then, it's hard."

*"A man has to think a long time before
he makes up his mind to cut a tree like this."*

With a quick pull on the cord, the saw started. Jed ran some distance away, in order to get out of falling range.

The motor roared as his father began the cut at the base of the tree. He notched it on one side, then went to the opposite side and cut. At first the tree stood erect. Then it began to lean, and finally, with a loud cracking noise, it thundered downward through smaller trees and brush. The final crash resounded through the hills as it settled to the ground.

Jed helped with the trimming and cutting of the logs. The load was completed, the binder tightened, and Dad was ready to leave for the mill.

"I'm going to look for a Christmas tree while you're gone, maybe back at the swamp."

"It's a sunny day. You shouldn't have any trouble," replied his dad, "but don't be too long. We have to get busy right away on the next load."

Jed started off toward the Christmas tree swamp. There was no worry. Long ago his father had taught him to take his bearings from the sun. With the deep covering of snow, it was a quiet day in the woods. Even his own footsteps made no noise. Jed stopped to enjoy the silence, then set out again.

Cresting the last small rise, he looked down on the swamp below. It was like a fairyland. Each evergreen branch was laden with snow, burdened almost to the ground. Reluctant to disturb the beauty, Jed waited for several minutes before he cautiously ventured among the trees.

With the ax handle, he tapped the trunk of a small tree, and the snow slid like an avalanche. Without warning, a wild commotion broke loose, snow flying and branches snapping. Startled, Jed fell to the ground in amazement.

4

A Glimpse of the Big One

A HUGE BUCK raced past him, almost trampling him into the ground. His gigantic rack of horns caught the evergreen branches in all directions. As Jed whirled to see, the frightened animal leaped high in the air and disappeared into the woods.

Instantly Jed knew that it was the Big One. He had been caught napping, but even in fright he was a magnificent animal, broad, straight, and proud.

Wild with excitement, Jed ran to the other side of the evergreen where the big buck had been sleeping, only ten feet from where he stood. The snow was melted, and Jed knelt to lay his hand flat in the bed. It was still warm, the biggest deer bed he had ever seen.

His imagination soared. Why not? he thought. His father had said that he could hunt, and come next season he would get the Big One!

He pictured what it might be like, bringing him home with all the family gathered and full of praise for his achievement. All he needed was a rifle. He could take care of the rest.

It was several minutes before Jed regained his senses and remembered why he had entered the swamp. He got to his feet and brushed the snow off himself.

He renewed his search for the tree, though he had trouble keeping his mind on the task. Tapping the trunk with the ax handle to remove the snow, he walked around several trees, making a close inspection. He wanted one that was thick and full so that it would cover the entire end of the living room. Finally he made his choice. It was a beautiful spruce, full on every side, and thick with cones.

Jed counted as he swung. It took 22 swings to bring it down. If I were a spruce, he thought, I'd like being a Christmas tree.

With the ax in one hand and the butt of the tree in the other, Jed started back to the logging area, pulling the tree behind him.

He wondered where the Big One had gone, and for a moment considered tracking him. No, he decided. The business at hand is the logging.

He had just returned to the landing and propped the tree in a snowbank when he heard the truck. He was glad he had not kept his father waiting. For the moment, he decided to say nothing about seeing the Big One.

"Looks like you found a beautiful tree, Son."

"Think they'll like it?"

"You know they will. It's a beauty."

His dad resumed the cutting, and Jed skidded one log after the other. The woods were filled with the sound of harvesting timber and the smell of working horses. Though he had stripped down to one shirt, Jed did not realize the pace they were keeping.

"Time for lunch," his father called. "It's a good thing we can't go this steady all the time. We'd have the whole woods cut in a week."

Now that he thought about it, Jed was hungry too. They sat down on one of the skidded logs.

"Better put your jacket on, Son, so you don't get chilled."

Jed leaned back and reached for the jacket, draping it around his shoulders.

"I don't know when your mother's roast beef sandwiches ever tasted better." Dad unwrapped another.

"Or her chocolate cake," Jed added. But even the chocolate cake, Jed's favorite, could not make him forget his recent experience. "Dad," he said finally, "when I was back at the swamp this morning, I saw the Big One."

His dad took a swallow of hot coffee. "You sure about that?"

"I'm sure."

"Well, Jed," he said, "I think that's something to

33

forget for the time being, but to keep in the back of your mind."

Jed was satisfied. Though he had not put it in words, that was pretty much the way he felt about it.

"I've got some news, too," Dad said. "The price on these logs has gone up—a lot. Seems to be more snow in most parts, and a lot of fellows can't get their logs out of the woods."

"That's great, Dad. The price, I mean."

"I don't intend to tell your mother. We'll let her have a surprise when she sees the check."

They went right at the loading, his dad running the tines of the loader under each log and raising it, while Jed held it with the cant hook to keep it from sliding off.

"Be careful," his dad said. "This logging is dangerous business. We've already had one close call. A man wouldn't stand a chance if one of these logs fell on him."

Jed reminded himself constantly to be cautious. As each log was placed on the truck, he was on top of the load with the cant hook to stop the log from rolling off the other side of the rack.

One log rumbled across fast. As Jed tried to stop it, it twisted the hook with force, throwing him off the load and onto the ground. He rolled over a couple times and then jumped up to escape if the log fell, but it stayed on the truck.

His dad was at his side, grabbing him by the

arm. "You all right, Son?"

"I'm OK," Jed answered, "just a little dizzy."

"We'll slow down. If you see you can't stop one, just get out of the way. We can always pick it up again."

A few more logs was all the truck could handle. "This will be it for today," his dad said. "I'm on my way."

"See you back at the house!" Jed called. He rounded up the equipment, hooked the horses to the sleigh, and put his tree on the top.

Jed whistled all the way home. It made a fellow feel good when he accomplished a lot. He thought of what Gretchen might say when she saw the tree.

Arriving at home, he was not disappointed.

"A tree!" shouted Gretchen. "A Christmas tree!"

"Oh, Jed, it's the most beautiful tree." Sari held the door open.

"It's gorgeous, but so huge!" exclaimed his mother. "We'll never have enough decorations."

"We'll make them," cried Sari. "Please don't say he has to take it out."

"Of course he doesn't have to take it out. I thought maybe we could take a little off the bottom."

"Where did you get it, Jed?" Jared asked.

" 'Way back at the Christmas tree swamp. It was just the one I was looking for."

When Dad came home later, his arrival was unnoticed in all the excitement that still filled the

"Oh, Jed, it's the most beautiful tree."

house. "Hey!" he called. "What's all the noise about?"

"We've got a Christmas tree," said Gretchen. "Come and see."

The evening was filled with joyous activity. At the Craig home, it was the children who did the Christmas decorating.

"Lift me up, Daddy," begged Gretchen, "so I can put this one 'way up there."

"Hold stiff," he said, hoisting her high.

"Jed, help me cut these stars," Sari said.

Hot grease sputtered in the kitchen later as Sari popped corn and then strung fluffy white ropes to encircle the tree.

Jed was thrilled. The tree looked just as he had imagined.

"Now can we hang up our stockings?" asked Gretchen.

Jed smiled. "It's too early for that. But we could put our manger scene on the hearth, couldn't we, Mother? All but the baby Jesus figure."

"It would be a wonderful time for that." She took a box from the high cupboard above the refrigerator and carefully unwrapped the figures, rolled in cotton.

Jed placed spruce boughs around the cotton base and gently set each figure in place.

"Mother," said Gretchen, "tell us what happened on Christmas night."

"On that night," Mother said, "God sent His only

37

Son into the world to bring love and peace to those who would accept Him. He was born in a manger, much like this one."

Gretchen sighed. "I can hardly wait. Do you think I could hold the baby?"

"I'll tell you what, Gretchen," Jared said. "It's my turn to put the baby in the crib on Christmas Eve, but I'll let you do it. That way you'll get to hold it."

"Oh, good." She gave him a tight hug.

"One more thing," said Jed's mother. She brought out a red Christmas candle, put it in a two-foot gold holder, and set it near the manger scene. By tradition, when lighted on Christmas Eve, the candle signaled the beginning of their family Christmas celebration.

"Come on, Gretchen," she said. "Time for bed."

"Sari, couldn't you put her to bed," Jed asked, "and give Mom a break?"

"Just walk up with her," said Mother. "Come on, Sari, Jared, it's time for you too."

When the smaller children were in bed, Dad pulled a paper from his pocket and winked at Jed. "How would you like to see this, Mother?" It was the check for the logs.

Mother unfolded the check. "John, it's more than half again of what we expected! Did you see this, Jed?" She held the check out toward him.

Jed was surprised at the amount, too, and happy.

"You two men are really something," she said.

"You know that? The children certainly won't be disappointed now."

"It's going to take more than that to pay the back bills," Dad said, "but with these prices, and if Jed and I can do some more cutting during vacation, things ought to be looking up around here."

Curled up in his bed later, Jed pulled the warm quilt over his ears. It had been a good day. Happiness filled the house, and with the extra money, he thought, maybe—just maybe—there would be a rifle for Christmas.

5

The Greatest Christmas Ever

ON MONDAY, Jed was back in school. He liked school and most of his classes, except for math. Woodworking was the best. But the aura of anxious excitement before the Christmas holiday made it hard to settle down to the bookwork.

The last day before vacation there was a class party, with the exchanging of gifts, and Christmas cookies and hot cocoa for lunch.

As they boarded the school bus it was snowing big flakes, wet and heavy.

"Boy, am I glad to be out of that place for a while," said Emery. He plopped down in a seat of the bus and flicked the snow out of his hair.

"You said it," Jed answered. "A little time away is just what I need."

"Are you going to have to work all during vacation?"

"No, not all the time. Maybe we could get together for some skating."

Emery slouched in the seat and looked out the window. "Who'd clean the snow off the ice?"

"We could."

"And work ourselves until we're too tired to skate?" He winked at one of the girls who had turned to look his way.

"You really think we'd be that bad off?"

"How about a sleigh ride instead?"

Jed changed the subject. "If it keeps snowing like this," he said, "we won't even be able to get out the door by morning."

"Hey, you're not kidding!" Emery sat up to take notice. "You can hardly see our house."

The driver slowed to a stop.

"Well, I got home anyway." Emery laughed. "With a little luck, maybe you guys will spend your vacation on the bus."

Right now, Jed failed to see too much humor in Emery's wisecracking. It was already difficult to see, and the visibility was worsening every minute.

"Do you think we'll get home, Jed?" Sari was straining to see the shoulder of the road.

"Sure, we'll get there. It's only a couple more miles."

It was almost impossible to keep the windshield

cleared. "I've been on these routes for a long time," the driver told Jed, "and I don't think I've ever seen this much snow come down in this short a time. If it was just you and Jared, I'd ask you to walk the rest of the way, but I don't think the girls could make it."

"No, I don't think they could," agreed Jed. "Besides, I don't know where you'd get turned around." The Craig house was the last stop on the route, and the remaining miles were one hill after the other.

It was slow, heavy going, but finally they turned in the driveway. Jed swung down off the bus. "I hope you get back to town all right," he said, "and have a happy Christmas."

His eyes swept the yard. Everything he could see was laden with white. A high fluff of cotton candy covered the top of each fence post, and clinging snow had changed the thin wires to heavy ropes. A branch from the huge evergreen across the driveway had snapped under the tremendous weight and lay in a covered bulk on the ground.

Jed tramped through the snow with the girls and Jared behind him. Even the short walk wore heavily on his legs. He stamped his feet on the porch to clear the snow.

"Oh, I thank God that you're home," Mother exclaimed. "The bus was late, and I was beginning to worry."

The snow-covered countryside was still beautiful, but within an hour a cold wind began to howl from the north, and by bedtime it had provoked a full-scale blizzard. Jed turned on the yard light and looked out the front window. Snow swirled around the corner of the house in blinding drifts. At the height of a gust, none of the outbuildings were visible. The windows of his room rattled and shook.

All night the storm raged, piling the snow into heavy solid mounds. When daylight came, the field to the west appeared to stretch clear to the lake— there was no sign whatever that a road had separated the two. Outside Jed's window, the maple tree stood in snow above the halfway mark. Even the door had to be forced open so that the porch could be cleared.

Going to the barn, Dad waded in snow nearly to his waist, and Jed followed in his tracks. At every step, he had to lift his leg over the mass in front of him and set it into the snow. There was no way to push through.

Weary, Dad stopped to survey the area. "This snow will put a stop to our logging," he said. "We couldn't possibly get around in the woods now."

Jed knew what that meant. "How will we ever pay the bills then?" he asked.

Dad breathed deeply, shaking his head. "We'll just have to cut back where there's any possible way, and do the best we can."

Jed wondered about the rifle. He wanted to ask,

but he knew by the look on his father's face that he was under great pressure. He remained silent.

The farm chores seemed to take longer than ever that Christmas Eve. Jed thought they would never be finished, but as he and his father walked across the yard to the house he saw that they had actually finished earlier than usual.

"Boy, time sure drags along when you're waiting for something," he said.

When they came into the kitchen, Jed saw that Mother and Sari had been hard at work, too. The table was covered with the lace tablecloth that was saved for special occasions. There were candles, too, and a centerpiece sprayed with gold glitter that Sari had made. It looked so warm and cheerful that Jed felt like shouting out loud, but he ran to wash and change instead.

"Hurry up, slowpoke!" Gretchen called. "We're all waiting for you."

As the family gathered in the living room, Jed looked around proudly. Everyone was dressed in his best. The Christmas candle and the lights of the tree, the only lights on, brightened the room with a soft glow. And he wished that Christmas came more than just once a year.

Dad began by reading the Christmas story from Luke. "And it came to pass in those days, that there went out a decree from Caesar Augustus..."

Jed could have almost repeated the familiar story from memory. The grand phrases came one

45

after another: ". . . unto the city of David, which is called Bethlehem . . . she brought forth her first-born son . . . a Saviour, which is Christ the Lord . . . Glory to God in the Highest . . ."

Then they all sang, even little Gretchen, though she didn't know all the words. As they sang "Silent Night" Gretchen was supposed to put the figure of the Christ child in the manger by the tree. But she had forgotten, so Jed poked her and she trotted over, a little awed.

As they sang "Joy to the World," the last song, Jed could feel the happiness around him. When the song was over the whole family hung their stockings.

"I hope Santa brings me one of those new dolls," Gretchen piped.

"You have so many already," Sari teased, "what could you do with one more?"

And Gretchen began to explain why the new doll was special in such a serious way that they all couldn't help laughing.

"Supper's ready," Mother called from the dining room.

They had their traditional Christmas Eve fish chowder, hot buns, and Christmas cookies, with a dessert of strawberry and sour-cream gelatin.

"Your mother, children, is one of the best cooks I know," sighed Dad. And he winked at Mother across the table.

"I did some of the cooking, too," said Sari.

"I did, too," said Gretchen. And the whole family laughed, just because it was so much fun to be together on Christmas Eve.

Fortunately, the roads were cleared by the time they had to leave for church.

As they were driving home later, after the midnight service, Jed looked out the window of the car at the white brightness of the snowbanks sliding smoothly by, and he thought, "This is the greatest Christmas Eve ever. Christmas will be perfect this year . . . if I get my rifle."

A shadow of worry crept across his happiness, but he pushed it away. After all, he had worked for the rifle. He went to sleep that night dreaming of sleek metal and the smell of gun oil.

6

A Setback

GRETCHEN WAS THE FIRST to awaken on Christmas morning, and within minutes the entire household was bustling with excitement.

She pulled Jed by the arm. "There's a package under the tree with my name on it. May I open it?"

"Wait until Mom and Dad get here. They'll be right out."

The stockings were filled with candy, nuts, oranges, and apples, and under the tree were gifts. Jed could wait no longer. He was down under the tree with the other children.

There was a long obvious package for Jared, a big heavy one for Sari, and a foot-square box for Jed. Disappointment filled his chest. He fought to choke back the tears, staying on the floor behind the rocker where no one would see. Why, for just once, couldn't things turn out right for him?

49

Gretchen hung forward over his shoulder. "Jed, look at my doll." She shrieked with delight. "And she can talk!"

Jared was overjoyed with his skis, and Sari, completely unsuspecting, exclaimed at the sight of a sewing machine, "I just can't believe it!"

Jed couldn't believe it either. He was sure the sewing machine must have cost at least as much as a rifle. But that was for Sari!

"I knew you would enjoy it, Sari," his mother said, "now that you've learned to sew at school. Perhaps it could be used for the family, too."

"Of course it can," said Sari. "I can hardly believe it."

Jed laid his head back against the rocker and tried to squeeze out the bitterness, but it was so unfair.

Then he heard his father. "Aren't you going to open your package, Jed?"

Jed took the box and untied it slowly. It was a small electric sabre saw. "This is really nice." He tried to sound convincing, and he thought no one guessed.

"You do so well in woodworking class," his mother said. "I'm glad you like it."

Jed placed the saw back in the box and set it on the floor beside him. His heart ached. Christmas had always been happy until this time.

Discarded paper lay all around. "If mess is any indication of a successful gift-giving," said Mother, "this was certainly successful. Come help me, Sari. The relatives will arrive in a few hours."

Christmas or not, there were still farm chores to be done. Jared hurried on ahead so that he could finish quickly and try his skis.

Jed and his father walked to the barn together. "I know what you were looking forward to, Son, and you had a right to expect the rifle. I realize how disappointed you are, even though you know why it wasn't possible."

Jed looked straight ahead.

"You do understand that I had to take some of the money for bills?"

He nodded.

Dad put his arm around Jed's shoulders. "There are several months left before hunting season. Don't you worry, Son. We'll get a rifle somehow."

Knowing that his father understood did help Jed some, and he was glad that the others did not know. But still a hopeless feeling gnawed at his stomach. He didn't see much chance for the rifle.

As the chores were finished, the relatives had already started to arrive. Uncle George, his father's brother, had brought Jed's grandmother and grandfather in his car. The two men carried his grandfather into the house while Jed followed with his wheelchair. He opened the chair, and they carefully set his grandfather down.

Granddad looked small in the chair, though Uncle George teased him about being heavy. He still had a full head of white hair and a look of dignity about him.

"I'll push you in by the tree, Granddad," Sari said. "Jed got it for us. It's just beautiful."

Granddad's eyes brightened. "Say, now, that is a dandy."

More relatives arrived, and the house was soon filled with aunts, uncles, and cousins. The women fussed over the dinner while the men talked and played games with the children.

When everyone was seated, Granddad asked the blessing. "We thank You, Lord," he said, "first for family, for the blessing of being together on this Christmas Day and sharing our joy with one another. We thank You for good health and for hearty appetites to enjoy the meal of which we are about to partake. We ask You to bless this food and to watch over us on each following day so that we may always remain under Your guiding care. We ask in Jesus' name. Amen."

Bowls of steaming hot mashed potatoes, topped with melting butter, were carried to the table, then bright red cranberry molds, golden squash, and fluffy white buns. But it was the venison rump roast, smothered in onions, that was the center of the holiday dinner, especially for the men.

"Here it comes!" said Uncle George. "I've been waiting for this ever since last Christmas." He took a generous helping. "Um, best venison roast I ever tasted," he said after his first mouthful.

"It's just that it's the most recent," said Jed's mother modestly.

"No siree," he said. "John always picks a good one, better every year. And with a good cook like you at the stove, it just can't be beat."

Mother was embarrassed. She glanced at Jed. "Jed's going to be hunting with John next year," she said.

All eyes shifted, and Jed felt 30 pairs of eyes trained on him. "Well, in that case," said Uncle George, "I'll just bet next year's roast will put this one to shame, delicious as it is."

A red blush rose in Jed's neck and covered his face. Why had his mother raised the subject? How could he hunt? He didn't even have a gun. Right now, he didn't even want to think about next year.

It was early evening, after the household quieted, when Emery stopped at the Craig house. Jed had gone to his room and was reading the directions included with the sabre saw. He thought of starting a gun rack, but that seemed so useless.

A knock sounded at his door, and Emery plowed in. "I couldn't wait to show you!" he blurted. He held up a rifle.

Jed felt as though he'd been kicked in the stomach. Emery almost never did anything constructive, and yet everything went his way. In a blur, Jed saw that it was an automatic. He heard Emery say "Remington." There was a scope, and fancy carving on the stock.

"Boy, I can't wait till hunting season." Emery was talking full speed, but Jed heard little.

Dad came in, and Emery raced through the description again.

"It's a handsome rifle, Emery," Dad said. "I don't blame you for being proud of it."

Emery started toward the door. "I have to be going. Dad's waiting in the car. I'm going over to show it to Gerald."

Jed raised his hand in good-bye.

They sat on the edge of the bed, Jed and his father.

"I know there's little I can say, Son, except that you and your mother and the family mean more to me than anything that can be bought or sold, and that more often it's the disappointments of life, rather than the joys, that make people strong." He put a hand on Jed's shoulder. "But it takes a lot of soul-searching to come around to that kind of thinking."

7

Commotion

LATE IN JANUARY, a new situation invaded the Craig household. Jed's father called the oldest children together.

"Boys, Sari, your grandmother is seriously ill. We've decided that Mother will go and stay with her and Granddad. We live the nearest, outside of Uncle George, but he and Aunt Liz have the new baby, and she can't be left."

"Isn't Grandmother in the hospital?" Jed asked.

"No," said his father. "She doesn't want to go to the hospital. And though she's very sick, the doctor says she can be cared for just as well at home."

"How did she get sick?" Sari asked.

Her mother explained. "It's not something that happened overnight. She's been caring for your grandfather for a long time. Though she wouldn't have it any other way, it has been heavy work, and Grandmother is not a young person."

"Did the doctor say what's wrong with her?" asked Jed.

"He said that she had a stroke."

Jed did not really understand, though he had heard of a stroke.

"Sari will do the cooking," Mother continued, "but I'm asking you to help her with other work in the house, Jed."

"How long will you be gone?" he asked.

"I wish I could tell you, but I don't know. I do know this is going to be hard for all of us, but difficult times come to everyone; and when they do, we simply do our best to handle them."

"When will you be going?"

"I'll drive your mother down tonight," Dad answered.

"So soon?"

"This is when your grandparents need help. When I get your mother there, we'll get things organized, and then I'll come home."

Jed did not enjoy supper. He felt lonely already. Except for once when she had been ill in the hospital, his mother had always been there, when he went to bed and when he awoke. He wasn't certain what it would be like without her, but he was certain he wasn't going to like it.

After supper, Jed helped his father in the barn. When they came in, his mother had already packed a small bag.

"I've written instructions for Sari, Jed. I hope

they help both of you. Please try to do what she asks."

"I will, Mother."

"And when you say your prayers," she said, "please ask God to watch over your grandmother in a special way."

After their parents had left, Jed and Jared made popcorn, and then they all ate it quietly in the living room. Feeling the loneliness, too, Gretchen curled up on the sofa near Jed and laid her head in his lap.

How different this was from the other evenings they'd spent. Instead of talk and laughter, there was somber silence. Even with the others in the room, Jed felt alone and uncertain.

When Gretchen fell asleep, Jed gathered his sister in his arms and carried her to bed. Sari and Jared followed him up the stairs. Carefully Jed covered her and pulled the door almost closed.

Sari waited in the hall. "It's a lot different without Mother and Dad here, isn't it?"

"It sure is."

"I don't like it," confessed Jared.

"Neither do I," Sari said.

"It'll be better in the morning," Jed told them. "Dad will be home then."

Jed went downstairs to his own room. Except for his parents' room, his was the only bedroom on the first floor, and he had always been fond of the quiet, but tonight he could not rest easily. The house was not as warm and comforting as before. There were many noises, inside and out, and many thoughts troubled him.

His father awakened him in the morning. "Jed," he said, shaking him gently, "time to fix breakfast."

Time to *fix* breakfast, thought Jed. Morning had always meant time to *eat* breakfast. Then he remembered. He hustled out of bed and pulled on his clothes.

Sari was in the kitchen, looking as sleepy and lost as he felt. "I can't even find the paper with the directions Mother wrote for me. I thought I left it in the kitchen, but I can't remember."

They both looked. "Here it is," said Jed, "under this pan."

"Oh, good. It tells how to make the cream of wheat. Jed, you get jam from the basement and start making toast. You have to put it in the broiler."

Sari started the cream of wheat, as well as the coffee, according to directions. Jed put the bread in the broiler and turned the stove on. Then he ran to the basement.

Sari was pouring the dry cereal into the water when suddenly Gretchen began screaming in the bathroom.

"What's the matter with her?" called Jed.

"I don't know. What is it, Gretchen?" Sari started for the bathroom.

Sari started the cream of wheat,
and Jed put the bread in the broiler to toast.

A hiss erupted from the stove as the cream of wheat boiled over. Sari grabbed for the pan. "Oh, my hand!"

Jed flew into the kitchen. "Put it in cold water!" He snatched a holder and jerked the pan off the burner.

Shrieking, Gretchen ran through the doorway, blood dripping from her hand. Jed grasped her by the wrist and stuck her hand under the faucet.

"Oh, no!" Sari screamed. "The toast!"

She whirled around to see smoke and flames coming from the oven. She grabbed the toast with her bare hands and flung it in the sink.

There was a mess all over.

Jed was trying to tend to Gretchen. With the blood cleared, he saw that she was cut, though not severely.

When their father came in, the coffee was perking out of the pot and over the counter, and Sari was scraping the burned crust from some of the toast.

His father unplugged the pot first. "I think you filled it too full."

"I guess," said Jed without looking up. He scraped with fury.

His father waited.

Jed stopped scraping. He glanced up. "Gretchen started to scream," he said, "and just that quick everything went wrong. The cream of wheat boiled over, the toast went up in smoke, and well, you see the rest." He was thankful Jared didn't smart off.

"What was the matter with Gretchen?"

"She cut her hand. She was brushing her teeth and broke the glass. I thought she was half killed by the way she was yelling."

Dad looked at Sari. She was stirring a new batch of cream of wheat on the other side of the stove. He put his arm around her. "I think that can come off now."

Then he started to grin slowly. "Won't we have a time telling your mother about this morning? She'd feel terrible if she thought we could get along without her. This is going to be a real boost to her morale."

Jed sulked. "But it sure isn't doing much for mine."

His father was still grinning. "Aw, come on. All's well that ends well. Let's eat." He looked at Gretchen sitting calmly at the table. "One small girl, causing all that confusion."

Gretchen was surprised. "You mean I started all that trouble?"

They all laughed.

"You'd better finish getting ready for school," Dad said, "or you'll miss the bus. I'll finish up."

After the morning's commotion, Jed decided that school was a snap. He was almost relieved to get there, and even math class was welcome. But the day seemed short.

When he arrived home, the household was calm.

His father had a roast in the oven, and potatoes were cooking. "Come on, Sari," Dad called. "Jed can set the table, while we make the gravy."

Jed raised his eyebrows in surprise. "I didn't know you could cook, Dad."

"I used to do a little now and then, but nothing like your mother. We don't have any dessert, but we'll have to make do."

Jed opened a jar of pickles.

"I think I could make gravy by myself, Dad, now that I really paid attention," said Sari.

"Of course you could. It's just making sure that you know how it's done." Dad kept up the conversation to improve their spirits during supper. "Come on, Jared," he said when they were finished, "we'll escape to the barn. You know who gets stuck with the dishes."

Jed scraped and carried plates, while Sari put the leftovers away. Then he dried.

"Do you like to do dishes, Jed?" asked Gretchen.

"It's not so bad," he said, "and if you put the silverware away, it would be even better."

"I'll do it." She went to work like a beaver.

"Now," said Jed, "if you've picked up in the living room by the time I have the floor swept, we'll make some popcorn to eat later."

When their dad came in, Sari was on the floor, coloring pictures with Gretchen. "You older ones better do your homework," Father said. "Gretchen can read me a story from her book."

They ate the popcorn, but Gretchen began to whimper when it was time for bed. Her father took her up, and Sari went in to sleep with her.

What if Mother wasn't coming home? Jed wondered. Could we ever learn to get along without her?

His father looked lonely too. "I wonder how things are going with your mother and grandmother," he said.

"Maybe we'll hear from Mother tomorrow," said Jed. "How was Grandmother when you were there last night?"

"Not good, Jed. Not good at all, and your granddad was feeling pretty blue."

"It was awful here too."

"It's never easy when there's a change," Dad reflected. "I guess you can see that from your mother being gone. But we have to accept it. To accept change means to grow. Besides, there's little we can do. We'll leave the outcome to the Lord, and abide by His decision."

63

8

A Room for Granddad

ON FRIDAY, Mother came home. It was a warm homecoming, with the children surrounding her and clinging to her. Jed was not ashamed to clasp his mother in his arms. "We missed you, Mother," he said.

"And how I missed you children—and home." She took each one of them to her in turn, hugging them fondly.

But their joy was overshadowed by the news of their grandmother's death. They all sat quietly around the kitchen table while their mother spoke. "Your grandmother seemed to improve for a short while," she told them, "but then she began to weaken. Nothing the doctor could do made any difference. She died late last night. Your grandfather and I were with her."

Sitting near her mother, Gretchen's face was full

of wondering. "What does it feel like to die?" Her dark eyes searched her mother's face for an answer.

Mother took her smallest daughter's hand in hers. She remained silent for a long moment. "Do you remember," she began, "the night you fell asleep on the sofa, and while you were sleeping, Daddy came and carried you up to your own warm bed?"

Gretchen nodded.

"That's what it feels like to die. You wake up to find that you are in your own warm place in Heaven, the place where you belong because the Lord has readied it for you."

Gretchen looked at her Mother in quiet belief. "I'm glad for Grandma," she whispered.

"I'm glad for Grandma, too." Mother smiled. "Her whole life was spent in doing things for others, looking after her children, helping anyone in need, and in these last years, devoting all the energy she had left to taking care of Granddad, who had provided for her and their children all those earlier years."

The thought comforted Sari. "First Granddad took care of her, and then she took care of him."

"That's about the way it was," Dad answered. "It's up to the strong to help the weak. And most times, no one person is either strong or weak all of the time, so we take our turn as things work out."

Jed could not picture his grandfather as a strong

man. He had always known him to be in a wheelchair. "Was Granddad a strong man?" he asked.

"Yes, he was," his father answered. "He farmed
and logged to take care of his family, just like I'm
doing. But one day he had an accident at the mill.
That was before you were born, Jed.

"Your mother and I had been married only a
short time, and we were living in that little house
on the corner, where Merricks live now. Uncle
George had moved to town when he married, but I
had always enjoyed the farming and logging.
Watching things grow, whether corn or trees, was
like seeing a miracle every day, so I stayed to make
our living here alongside your granddad.

"Then the timber was bigger than what it is now.
Your granddad and I together couldn't reach
around some of the trees. On that particular day, it
was late when we had our load ready—big heavy
logs—so your granddad asked me to head on home
and start the farm chores while he went to the mill.
At that time, he used a set of fit hooks on the
wrapper chain to secure the load, one near the
front of the load, and one near the back. You
needed two men for unloading, one to loosen each
hook at the same time.

"He backed the truck into the unloading area,
planning to ask the man who would scale the logs
to unhook one. But the mill workers were already
leaving for the evening, and he didn't call to them.
He figured that the load was stacked square

67

enough so that the logs would stay in place until he unhooked the second log. But he misjudged. When he unfastened the front hook, the logs fell down over the edge of the rack. He dived under the truck, trying to escape, but he was crushed against the wheel below his waist. It was only by the grace of God that his life was spared. The doctors told him that he would never be able to walk again. Your granddad has accepted that injury with lasting patience, and he's been in the wheelchair ever since. That was when your grandparents moved to town and your mother and I took over the work here."

"What will happen to Granddad now?" asked Sari.

Father looked around the table. "That's the first thing we're going to discuss."

"He can come and live with us," Gretchen declared.

"I think that's what your father would like," Mother said. "But the family should decide together, since it would mean a change for all of us."

"It would be a big change for Granddad, too," Dad said.

"I think he will be awfully lonely," said Sari.

"He will," agreed her mother. "But if we could keep him from being too lonely, it's one return we could make for some of your grandmother's many kindnesses."

"I'd be willing to be more quiet," said Jared, "if I

had to, and I could help him in and out of his chair. He likes Mom's cooking."

Sari was eager. "Can he come, Dad?"

Dad rested his elbow on the table and brushed his hair to the side. "A lot depends on Jed," he said. "We'd have to ask him to give up his room and move upstairs with Jared."

Jed had wondered what room his grandfather might have.

"Because of the wheelchair," said Mother, "Granddad would have to have a downstairs room."

Jared spoke up. "That would be fun, Jed. We could lie and talk at night—if we were quiet about it."

Jed looked up at him. His face was smiling and eager.

One of Jed's greatest enjoyments had been a room of his own. He liked to sit in the quiet and think. And being downstairs near his parents, he had been allowed to share in many of the grown-up decisions affecting the household. Moving in with Jared would be a step backward.

Then he remembered the time when he was little and had the measles, and his mother had been sick and had gone to the hospital. Grandmother and Granddad had come, Granddad in his wheelchair, to care for him and Sari. He didn't remember where his grandparents had slept then, or even if they had slept.

He raised his eyes and looked from one to the other. There was nothing else to do. "If Jared can cram his belongings into half of that room," he said, "I guess I can cram mine into the other half."

"Oh, good!" cried Gretchen.

Mother and Jared smiled approvingly, but there were tears of joy in their father's eyes. "Thanks, children. It means a lot to me." He rubbed a rough hand across his eyes. "One day I came to your granddad's house," he said. "That was the day I was born. He made room for me, and I stayed for better than 20 years. I'm glad we can make room for him this time around."

"And isn't it lucky," said Gretchen, "that Granddad will be here in time for my birthday? That should make him happy."

Dad patted her on the head. "I'm sure he'll be very happy about your birthday, Gretchen."

9

A Winter Picnic

A FEW DAYS after Grandmother's funeral, Mr. and Mrs. Craig drove into town to get Granddad and bring him home.

While they were gone, Jed gathered his things together and prepared to move upstairs to Jared's room.

"I'll help you carry your things up," Jared said. "I've got my stuff all taken care of."

Jed knew that Jared had made his room ready as soon as the decision had been reached. He was excited about the new arrangement, and Jed was glad that Jared did not know how much he hated to give up his privacy.

"I could use a hand with this dresser. The bed is going to stay here for Granddad."

"Mom set up that other single bed in my room—I mean *our* room. I even cleaned out the closet in your honor. Don't you think it's going to be fun?"

"I suppose it'll be OK," said Jed, "but once in a while I like it really quiet. So if you can remember that, I guess we'll get along all right."

"And I thought it was Granddad I was going to have to be quiet for."

"Don't worry," said Jed, "it won't be all the time."

When his parents returned with Granddad, Jed and his father carried the older man into the house and put him in his chair.

"When spring comes," Dad said, "Jed and I can build a ramp so that you can get out in the sunshine and look around the place."

"And I'll wheel him," said Gretchen. "It's going to be my birthday in a few days. Aren't you glad you got here for it?"

"I sure wouldn't want to miss out on a birthday cake," Granddad answered.

"Jed moved up with Jared so you can have his room," Gretchen said, "and he hopes Jared shuts his mouth sometimes so he can think."

"Gretchen!" Jed's face turned bright red. "I never said that!" He didn't want to make his grandfather feel unwelcome.

But the words seemed to bounce right off Granddad. "Don't worry about it, Son," he said. "I'm a thinker myself. Your folks brought my big chair along, and that's where I'll be doing my thinking, so there'll be plenty of room on the bed for you. Two thinkers aren't about to bother each other."

Granddad had a way of easing things. "Thanks, Granddad," Jed said. "I just may be taking you up on that."

Mother brought in Granddad's clothes and hung them in the closet. "Jed," she asked, "would you bring in those few boxes from the car and put them in that green cupboard on the back porch?"

"Don't you want them in your room, Granddad?"

"No. Those are just a few old things that I'll never use, but I hate to part with. I asked your mother to store them someplace out of the way."

Jed brought the boxes to the porch and put them in the cupboard.

The next several days were spent with everyone showering attention on the new member of the household. It reminded Jed of the day in fourth grade when a new girl came to school. Everyone buzzed like bees all day; but besides wearing themselves out, no one got anything done. He hoped that things would soon settle down to normal.

One evening Granddad wheeled himself into his room early and closed the door. Gretchen was coloring pictures on the floor while Sari and Jared were arguing over a game they were playing.

If the door had been left open, it would not have bothered Jed. But closed, it signaled an invitation to shut out noise and activity. He hesitated a moment and then opened the door, entered, and closed it. Granddad, sitting by the window, did not look up. The bed was empty and Jed sat down on the edge. It felt like home. He lay back on the pillow with his hands behind his head, as he'd done so many times before, and closed his eyes. He breathed deeply to relax. Oh, was it ever good to think in that room! Jed wondered if everyone had a special place for thinking. He thought of the past and the present, but mostly of what was still to come. An hour or perhaps more had passed when he realized he was becoming tired. His grandfather must be too, he thought.

Jed sat up and swung his legs to the floor. "Can I help you into bed, Granddad?"

"Yes, you can, Son, and thanks for the visit. It's the first good one I've had since I've been here."

"I enjoyed it," said Jed. "Things will settle down, I'm sure. Tomorrow is Gretchen's birthday. Everybody in the house will be waiting on her. That'll give you a little rest."

"In that case, I guess it is a good thing I got here for her birthday," Granddad said, and they both laughed.

Jared was already asleep when Jed went up to bed, and that night, for the first time, Jed did some thinking in the room they shared. He was certain that he and his grandfather understood each other, and he no longer felt so "moved out" of his own room. Having Granddad in the house was going to be all right.

The next morning was Saturday, and Gretchen's birthday. Birthday gifts were not usual in the Craig household, but everyone did all they could to make it a happy day for the birthday person, and that started with a chorus of "Happy Birthday" at the breakfast table.

"Do you have some special plans for your birthday, Gretchen?" her father asked.

"I decided," she answered, "that I would have Jed take me on a winter picnic."

"A winter picnic!" Mother exclaimed. "Where did you get an idea like that?"

"I read about one in our reading book at school," said Gretchen, "and I'm lonesome for a picnic, so I thought I'd have one for my birthday."

Mother looked at Jed hopelessly, but he was interested. "I don't know why not," he said, "if you can rustle up a picnic lunch."

His mother looked surprised. "Well, I can do that."

"OK, Gretchen," said Jed. "It's a date, as soon as I'm done with my chores."

Jed admired Gretchen's enthusiasm. Now that he'd heard of one, the idea of having a winter picnic sounded OK.

As soon as his chores were finished, Jed headed for the garage. He hunted until he found the pair of snowshoes that he'd seen his father use during other winters, and he brought out the small toboggan for Gretchen to ride on.

"So that's how you intend to handle it," his

father remarked.

"It should be all right, don't you think?"

"I think it'll be fine. I was wondering how you planned to get very far with Gretchen in all this snow."

"We won't go far," said Jed. "Just out of sight of the house. But I'm sure it will seem like a long way to her."

Gretchen was delighted. Mother had the picnic lunch ready, a thermos of hot chocolate, some hot dogs and marshmallows, and baked beans and banana bread.

"I don't think I'd mind a winter picnic by the looks of that," said Jared.

"Maybe another time," answered Jed, "when we see how this one turns out. Anyway, this is Gretchen's day."

Gretchen sat on the toboggan holding the lunch, and Jed started off on the snowshoes, pulling her behind. They went out across the front yard and started down the lake, from end to end.

It was a nice day for mid-February, not too cold, and the sun was shining brightly. As they neared the end of the lake, Jed swung into a little bay that put them out of sight of the house.

"What's that, Jed?" Gretchen pointed across the bay to the steep hillside where he and his father had nearly gone over the bank. There were two furry animals sliding down a worn trail on their tummies.

"Shhh!" he whispered. "Those are otters. I haven't seen them for quite a while and I wondered if they had left. Sit quiet and we'll watch."

After one of the otters reached the bottom of the slide, he ran back to the top of the hill and slid down again. Then he spotted Jed and Gretchen. The two animals tumbled a few times in the snow, and then both disappeared near the edge of the lake.

"Where did they go?" Gretchen asked.

"They live in a house in that bank. They have an opening down under the water and then a tunnel from there up to their house. There is also a land opening somewhere up the bank. Right now they disappeared down into the water. They keep a hole open somewhere in the ice. That's why you have to be careful of ice on a lake where otters are living. There could be an opening that you don't expect."

"What were they doing on that bank?"

"Just sliding. Otters are the most playful animals there are. They dive and catch fish, and slide in the snow and mud. That's why they're so much fun to watch."

"They sure are funny," said Gretchen. "I didn't think we would see any animals on my picnic."

"How about having the picnic now?" asked Jed. "I could build a fire here."

Gretchen looked around. "This looks like a good spot. OK. Let's have the picnic," Gretchen said. "I'm hungry."

Jed kicked away some of the snow with his boots to make a small pocket. Then he peeled some dry birch bark from a tree. He broke some small twigs and then some larger pieces from a dead maple, and arranged them in the pocket. Holding a match to the birch bark, he blew lightly. The twigs kindled quickly, and the wood blazed. Then he cut and trimmed two small green branches with his pocketknife.

Gretchen opened the bag and Jed threaded the hot dogs onto the ends of the trimmed sticks.

"If I had to be lost in the woods," said Gretchen, "I sure would want to be lost with you."

Jed laughed. "Especially if I had hot dogs and cocoa, I bet."

"I bet you could find something to cook."

"Maybe some game—an animal or a bird—if I had something to shoot it with."

"How about an otter?"

"No, I don't think they're any good to eat. I guess some fancy ladies like the skins for fur coats, but I'd rather wear an old coat and watch them slide and have fun."

"So would I, but when we come again," she added, "bring your gun so you can hunt some game."

"I don't really have a gun," Jed told her. "In fact, I don't have a gun at all. Dad did say I could go hunting with him next fall and that we'd have to get a gun, but I don't know how we'll be able to."

"You know how to shoot, don't you?"

"If I had to be lost in the woods, I sure would want to be lost with you," said Gretchen.

"Sure. I've used Dad's .22 lots of times."

"Can you shoot straight?"

"Straight enough to get what I see. Remember the squirrels I brought home?"

"You want a gun real bad, don't you?"

"Yes, I guess I do," said Jed. "How did you know?"

"Sari told me, and when you talk about a gun you look like Sari looks when she talks about having a boyfriend someday."

"You better eat your hot dog," said Jed, "before it gets cold." He had set the open can of baked beans in the red coals, and now they were bubbling. "Mittens make good potholders," he said. "Did you know that?" He took the hot can out of the coals and put it on the toboggan between them.

Gretchen passed him a spoon, and they both dipped into the beans.

"I didn't know a lot of things I found out about today," she said. "That's why it's fun out here with you."

"That's why I like to go out in the woods with Dad," Jed told her. "I learn about so many things, and it doesn't even seem like he's trying to teach me. It just comes out. It's different from school."

Gretchen sighed. "You're lucky you're a boy."

"You think so, huh?"

"Sure, you get to do all the fun things."

"But look who gets to pull and who gets to ride," Jed kidded her. "What do you have to say now?"

Gretchen wrinkled her nose and made a funny face at him.

"Come on," he said. "Let's pack this stuff up. Maybe you'll learn something more on the way home."

Jed told her what kind of a tree was the best for firewood, and which kind was the best for fence posts, and how to tell the difference.

"Is Jed ever smart," Gretchen told her father when they reached the house. "We had the best time. He told me all kinds of things about trees and otters. I'm going to have another winter picnic on my birthday next year."

"I just told her things that you've told me," said Jed.

"And things Granddad told me," added Dad.

"You mean Granddad knew all that first?" asked Gretchen. "Boy, Granddad, you must be really smart!"

"It's just that I've been around a long time, child," her granddad answered. "You can't live that long and not learn a few things."

10

The Big Mistake

BY EARLY APRIL Granddad was a family regular, and he and Jed had become good friends.

The weather was warming steadily, and the snowbanks shrinking fast. The dirt road past the Craig house, which had been frozen all winter, was heaving with frost boils, leaving it spongy and muddy.

"We nearly got stuck down at the corner," announced Jed when they arrived home from school one Thursday night. "Our driver is going to call the town chairman and see if he can't get something done about it. It isn't too bad in the morning when the surface is frozen again, but by late afternoon it's a mess."

"It'll be a while before it dries out," his father answered. "All that moisture has to go somewhere. Be sure you wear your boots. If you do get stuck and have to get out, at least you'll be prepared."

"I'm anxious to get some work done on the yard," Mother said. "After the snow melts, it looks so unkempt until it dries up and we can get it raked."

Dad smiled. "Spring is here for sure. Everybody's talking about what has to be done."

"Well, let's sit down," said Mother. "Supper is ready, and there's nothing I can do about the yard right now anyway."

During supper, the phone rang and Jed answered. "For you, Dad," he called. "The town chairman."

When he had finished talking, Jed's dad came back to the table. "He wanted to know if I could put the blade on the tractor and go over the road a few times to get it leveled off and dried out."

Mother sipped her coffee. "What did you say?"

"I told him I could if Jed would help me put it on in the morning before school. It's over in the shed, and we can't get there tonight because of that soft low area; but if it's frozen in the morning, we could manage. Then I could put on some additional weight and scrape it during the day."

"Can't he send the grader out?" asked Jed.

"The grader's too heavy for the road in the shape it's in. It'll have to be scraped with the blade several times first."

"Sure, I'll help you in the morning."

Early the next morning, before they left for the barn, Emery phoned.

"Dad," Jed called out, "Emery wants to know if we can ride our bikes to school this morning. The weather report says it's going to be warm and sunny."

Dad looked toward Jed's mother. "It seems silly to pedal in the mud when you can ride the bus," she said, "and you'd have to leave so early to get there."

Jed put his hand over the mouthpiece. "It'll be frozen this morning, and it's only three miles to the blacktop. By the time Dad scrapes it today, it'll be in pretty good shape, especially off to the sides."

His mother remembered. "That's right," she said. "You promised to help Dad put the blade on this morning. You can't possibly leave early."

"We can still get that done if we hurry. Please, Dad?" Jed was really pleading now.

Dad recognized Jed's spring fever too. "Tell you what," he said, "if we get the blade on and you fuel up the tractor for me so I can start grading right after chores, you can go ahead and ride the bike to school."

"Thanks, Dad." Jed put the phone back to his ear. "Emery, I can leave in about 25 minutes. OK?" He paused. "All right, see you then."

"Twenty-five minutes!" His mother was indignant. "You won't have time to eat any breakfast."

Jed shrugged his shoulders. "I'm not that hungry anyway."

"Well, you can't go without breakfast. A growing boy needs nourishment."

"Then pack me some toast and oranges. I'll eat when I get to school."

"What kind of a breakfast is that?"

Dad sided with Jed. "Once in his life won't hurt him, Mother. A growing boy has to do something a little out of the ordinary now and then, too. You know the old story about all work and no play."

"All right," she said, "if you say so," but she still looked doubtful.

"Come on, Dad," called Jed. "We're wasting precious time."

"Aren't you going to have your coffee before you go, John?"

"Later. When you want them to help, you have to do it their way some of the time."

Jed was out of the house and on the tractor. He had it backed up to the front end of the scraper blade when his father got there. Together they lifted one side of the blade, putting blocks under it until it reached the height of the drawbar. Then they raised the other side.

"Back her up a little more, Jed."

Jed jumped on the tractor and backed it a few inches so that the drawbar was directly in line with the mounting plate of the scraper.

Quickly they secured the bolts in place. "There, that didn't take long," said his dad. "I'll run and start the chores. You fuel it up and then you can go." He started toward the barn. "Check the gauge, too, will you? I'll be starting in the field as soon as it dries up, and if there's not enough gas, I'll have to call for the truck to bring some."

"OK, Dad, I'll let you know."

Jed started the tractor and drove toward the gas barrel. Cranking the wheel tightly as he made the corner, he brought it in close enough so that the hose would reach.

He hopped off the tractor and onto the metal stand that held the barrel about ten feet off the ground. Grabbing the nozzle end, he stuck it into the gas tank on the tractor, then opened the valve to let the gas run in. He remembered to check the gauge—123 gallons it said.

He blocked the nozzle handle open with a stick and ran to the barn while the gas was flowing. "Dad," he called, "the gauge says 123 gallons, so after I fill the tractor there'll be about 110 left."

"OK, Jed, thanks. That's enough for a start. Drive the tractor down by the house, will you?"

"OK, Dad. Bye."

Running back to the tractor, Jed checked his watch. He'd have to hurry. He took the stick from the handle and pulled the nozzle up to check the tank. It was nearly full. He decided to call that good. He closed the valve, hooked the nozzle end back on the stand, replaced the gas cap, and jumped on the tractor. Starting it instantly, he released the clutch and the tractor lurched forward. He heard a racket. Glancing back, his heart leaped. He had caught the stand with the protruding blade, pulling it over, and the barrel had plummeted to the ground.

Jed sprang from the tractor. The fill hole was on the bottom side, and the gas was running out. He pushed on the barrel with all his strength, but couldn't turn it. He tore for the barn.

"Dad!" he shouted. "Come quick! I tipped over the gas barrel!"

His father dropped a milk bucket and ran.

"It's lying on the fill hole."

"Get that pry pole around the corner. Hurry!"

Jed ran for it.

Jared saw him rush. "What's happened? You're white as a ghost."

Jed didn't answer. Pole in hand, he whirled and ran with Jared after him.

His father moved solemnly to one side. "No use," he said quietly. "It's empty." Then, with drooping shoulders, he walked slowly toward the barn.

Jared stared.

Jed held his forehead. He felt sick all over. He breathed deeply and pushed the air back out. "Jared," he said finally, "will you call Emery and tell him I can't make it?" He didn't look up.

"Should I tell him why?"

"Just tell him I can't make it, and tell the driver not to wait for me either."

Jared didn't ask any more questions.

Jed walked toward the barn. He wouldn't be going anywhere today.

That Friday was the longest day he'd ever spent. The tension was terrible. They finished milking in silence and ate in silence. No one even questioned his not going to school.

After breakfast, he trailed behind his dad to the gas barrel. They reerected the stand. His father picked up the barrel with the loader and set it back in place. The only words exchanged were the few necessary to do the work.

"I'm going to grade the road," Dad said then. "Ask your mother to call Fred for a fill. We can't be without gas when the fields are ready."

Jed walked to the house. He was sure he would feel better if he'd been beaten to a pulp, but that wasn't Dad's way.

The next morning when Mother came to the kitchen, Jed stood staring out the window.

She came and stood beside him. "What's the matter, Jed? Didn't you sleep last night?"

"No, I sure didn't. I hope I never have another day like that as long as I live."

"Jed, we all make mistakes. The important thing isn't that we've made one, but that we learn from it."

Head hanging, he picked at a scrap of paper on the floor with his bare toes.

"I think you've learned from this one."

Jed looked up. "I have. I'll never be careless enough to do a dumb thing like that again. I've been sick all over, Mom." He was near tears.

"I know you have, Jed." Her voice was filled with tenderness. "But there's one thing more you shouldn't overlook. The beauty of life is that every day is a new beginning."

"Then what could I do to make up?"

"It isn't so much the idea of 'making up,' Jed. Learning from a mistake is 'making up' for it." She studied his face. "But you still feel terrible. Is that right?"

Jed nodded. "I'd feel better if Dad had really chewed me out."

"No, you wouldn't, Jed. You've shown that you realize the consequences of your action. That's the better way. But now, how can you be happy again?"

Jed shook his head. "Yes, how?"

"Happiness comes, Jed, when you give happiness away. Decide on something you can do to make someone else happy. Think about it while you're milking. You'll come up with something."

11

The Ramp

AFTER BREAKFAST, Jared announced his intention of setting out with a shovel and pick to detour the seasonal streams as he saw fit. This always had been good spring sport for the boys, but this time Jed declined. "No," he said. "You go ahead without me. I have another project I want to start."

"OK," Jared called, "but you'll be missing out on a lot of fun."

"Dad," Jed asked, "would it be all right if I used some of that lumber in the shed?"

"What for, Son?"

"I thought I'd see what I could do about starting that ramp so Granddad can get outside without having to depend on us."

His dad brushed his hand through his heavy dark hair. "Jed," he said, "it's been hard for me to mention yesterday. It was a big loss. I can't deny that. But your mother told me you didn't sleep much last night. You've suffered enough. It's time we put it behind us, but I had to get it off my chest first." He reached over and shook Jed gently by the shoulder. "You're still the best hired man I ever had."

Jed smiled through watery eyes, but the lump in his throat kept him from speaking.

"I'll tell you what," his father suggested, "I'll give you a hand. The ramp would be a pretty big job for one man."

"That would be great. Do you think we could get it done today?"

"We'll have to wait and see on that one. Do you want to get the tools or start the figuring?"

"Get the tools; you do the pencil work."

Jed came back with the tools and looked at his dad's paper. "I guess it's a good thing I didn't try this by myself. I'd probably have it going up instead of down."

"I doubt that it would be that bad."

"One thing's for sure, you're better at math than I am." He sat down alongside his father, and together they figured the slant and the length of the ramp. Then the work began.

By noon they had a fair amount of the framework started. Mother called them for lunch just as Emery stopped by on his bicycle.

"Go ahead, Dad," Jed said. "I'll be there in a minute."

"How come all of a sudden you couldn't come yesterday, and then you didn't show up at school at all?"

"Something came up here," said Jed. "Something that couldn't wait, so I stayed to help Dad."

"How about going for the ride now?" asked Emery.

"It would be fun," admitted Jed. "I haven't even had my bike out yet this spring, but I can't leave this project now."

"Why not? You don't *have* to help, do you?"

"I'm not the one doing the helping," said Jed. "I wanted to build it, and Dad's helping me."

Emery took a closer look. "What is it, anyway?"

"It's a ramp, so my grandfather can wheel himself in and out of the house whenever he wants to."

"When you're that old," said Emery, "you don't even want to go outside anymore."

"Yes, he does. He likes to get out, but he hates to bother anyone to help him."

"Can't you do it next Saturday?"

"No," said Jed, "not this time. If you're interested in next Saturday for a ride, that looks better to me."

"Well, OK," said Emery. "I'll see if Gerald can go."

Sari had come to the door to see why Jed was not coming for lunch. She went back to the table. "Emery is out there coaxing Jed to go for a bike ride and forget the ramp," she told the others.

"Go ahead for a ride, Son," his grandfather said when Jed came in. "You've worried yourself enough over that episode yesterday. A little relaxation will do you good."

Jed was firm. "That's not the way I want it, Granddad," he said.

At chore time, the ramp was still unfinished, and Jed was disappointed.

"We could finish it after supper," his father said. "I'm not too tired to work a little longer, are you?"

"No," said Jed. "This kind of work is fun, because it's a work of kindness."

Dad did the sawing while Jed nailed the flooring on the ramp. In an hour and a half they were finished.

On Sunday afternoon, after they had come from church and eaten dinner, the whole family gathered to watch Granddad give the new ramp a try.

"Wait," said Sari, "we ought to have a ribbon-cutting ceremony," and she ran to get a ribbon saved from Christmas, and a pair of scissors. She tied the ribbon across the ramp railing at the porch. "Who wants to do the cutting?" she asked.

"I do!" cried Gretchen.

"It's customary to have a beautiful young lady doing such honors," Granddad said. "Do we have a pair of scissors?"

"Right here." Sari handed them to Gretchen.

Mother and the girls stood on the porch with

"It's customary to have a beautiful young lady doing such honors," Granddad said.

Granddad, while Jed, his father, and Jared stood at the bottom of the ramp.

Jared spoke up. "This ramp is dedicated to Granddad Craig, oldest living descendant of the Craig family who homesteaded this land almost a hundred years ago. Now for the cutting of the ribbon, Gretchen Craig!"

Gretchen cut the ribbon with one snip. There was a round of hearty applause.

"There will be a reception inside immediately following the first run," announced Mother. "We're serving cake and ice cream."

"That means Granddad has to make it back up," said Gretchen.

"Be careful, Granddad," said Jed. "You'd better hold back a little on the wheels."

"I bet he feels like he's trying for his driver's license," said Jared.

Granddad looked nervous. "I do," he confessed. "They say you can't teach an old dog new tricks."

"Just be careful, Dad," Jed's father warned. "It may take a few tries, but you'll soon get the hang of it."

"Do you want some help?" asked Jed.

"No, I don't want any help," Granddad said. "After you fellows worked out here so hard to rig this thing up, the least I can do is give it a try." He wheeled himself to the ramp. The front wheels started down the incline, but Granddad held them back by grasping the top of the big wheels and letting them slip through his hands a little at a time. The ramp curved to the right, and he let out more on the left wheel—just the right amount. Keeping the chair under control, he reached the ground safely.

A cheer rose from the whole family. "Yea for Granddad!" yelled Gretchen.

"He passed the test for his license!" shouted Jared.

Jed just smiled, but Granddad looked relieved. "You two did a good job," he said. "I appreciate this."

"Going up will be a little harder," Jed said. "I'll walk behind you for a few tries. It's going to take some power to do it."

"Follow me up then," said Granddad. It was somewhat of a struggle. Pushing both wheels at the same time was unsuccessful, as he lost ground when he tried for a new grip, and there was the danger of rolling backward. Finally Granddad found that rotating first one wheel and then the other in rhythm worked the best, but he was tired when he finally reached the top.

"It's going to work fine," he told Jed. "All I need now is practice. The exercise will strengthen my arms, too, and I'll be moving around real good before long."

"Then let's get to that ice cream and cake," Dad suggested.

Granddad was right. He practiced several times

a day, and by the following Saturday he could come up the ramp on his own.

Jed and Emery went off on their bike ride, and Jed felt good waving to his grandfather who was sitting in the spring sun, dreaming, no doubt, of what the growing season would bring.

The two boys pedaled along the country road and stopped to rest near a small trickling stream on the edge of the woods. The sun shone brightly on the moving water, sending out sparkles like flashing crystal.

With one hand, Jed motioned for silence. Upstream, a golden deer bent its graceful body to drink. The boys stood motionless, hoping to remain unnoticed. But sensing intruders, the deer raised its head, twitched its ears into an alert position, and with one flick of its white tail, darted into the woods.

"Wasn't that a beauty?" said Jed.

"That was really a nice one," agreed Emery. "Say, have you got a rifle yet?"

"Not yet."

"Do you know when you're getting one?"

Jed shook his head.

"I sure hope you do. It would be more fun if we could both go hunting."

"We couldn't go together anyway," said Jed. "We're too young to hunt without our dads."

"Phooey on that!" said Emery. "I'll hunt by myself if I want to."

"Not me," said Jed. "I think I'd better go by the rules. Of course, I'll be 13 this summer, and if I take the gun-safety course and pass, I could be hunting by myself in one more year."

"I don't intend to waste my time on that course," said Emery. "I've heard a lot of kids say you don't learn anything anyway."

"Well, I'm taking it," said Jed. "You can't be too careful."

"My dad's been talking about getting a new gun," said Emery, "and if he does, maybe you could buy the one he has now."

"Maybe so." Secretly, Jed hoped for a gun that was all his, right from the start, but he had to get a rifle of some kind if he was going to hunt at all. "I'll keep it in mind," he said.

12

Birthday Present

IN SPITE OF THE UNUSUAL AMOUNT of melting snow, the ground dried early that year; and with the spring work on the farm, the season was over before Jed had time to think about it. He and his father planted the oats, then plowed and worked the ground for corn. Jed helped every evening after school until dark. It seemed to him that morning after morning came just after he had laid his head on the pillow.

By the end of May, the corn and garden crops were planted, school was out for the summer vacation, and already Jed and his dad were beginning the harvest of the first crop of hay. It was a heavy crop, and they worked fast to take advantage of the hot and windy weather.

They needed rain, but no rain fell. In the weeks that followed, Jed watched the corn and garden plants wilt. The grass stood still, and, without pasture, the cows milked little.

Mornings and evenings were spent carrying pails of water from the lake to nourish the vegetables, berries, and flowers. Even the apple trees had to be watered, and each one needed more than the children could carry in an hour.

Jed became discouraged with the everlasting task.

"Some folks aren't nearly so well blessed," Dad reminded them. "We'd better thank the Lord that we have the lake to carry water from, and to cool us off and clean us, too."

It was easier for Jed to thank the Lord for swimming than for carrying the water. When he was wet and hot from work, nothing felt better than to dive off the big oak that lay out over the shoreline and feel the cool refreshing water flow over his face and body.

Jed was a good swimmer, and Sari watched him with admiration.

Mother saw the approval in her gaze. "I don't see why Jed couldn't teach you to swim," she said.

"Oh, could he?"

Jed was far from eager. "When it comes to anything athletic," he said, "Sari doesn't learn very fast." It looked to him like just one more job, a big one.

"That's why she needs your help," his mother replied.

Seeing that she wanted desperately to learn, Jed began the lessons.

"You have to remember, Jed," Mother said, "that Sari has never had a chance to be in the water, while you have been swimming every summer since you were big enough to walk. You must be patient with her."

Sari finally did learn to put her head under the water without filling up her mouth; and by hanging onto a limb of the oak, she developed a fair kick. But to coordinate a stroke and a kick seemed impossible.

"Relax, Sari," Jed told her. "I think you're trying too hard. You kick and thrash without any system. Slow down." Then they would have to quit for the day before Jed became too upset.

Each day he began the task again. "Look, Sari, breathe in and hold your breath. Then just lie in the water like this, as if you were going to rest." He lay in the water face down, his head under, hands straight at his sides, and his legs out. He was floating face down. The water was clear, so Sari could see perfectly what he was doing.

He stood up. "There," he said. "There's nothing to be afraid of, because you can always stand up."

"I'll try it," she said. She pulled in some air and relaxed, just as Jed had done. She was floating near the surface of the water like a buoy.

"I think you've got it," Jed said as she stood up.

"I have!" she yelled, the water still dripping from

103

her face. "It felt so wonderful, just like a dream."

"Now all you have to do," Jed said, "is to lie in the water like that, and when you've had time to think about it, start your kick. Try just that much for a few times. Then put in your stroke, and lift your head out of the water. If you manage even one stroke, you're on your way."

The system worked. "Jed is the greatest teacher," she told her father that evening. "Now all I have to do is practice. It's so much fun, the most wonderful thing I ever learned to do. I'm sure glad I have Jed for a brother."

"Quite a few folks around here are glad we have Jed," Dad said.

Jed had to admit that it was a good feeling to succeed with the lessons. He felt a new worth in himself, and he began to understand what his father had told him about the strong helping the weak.

But he felt a bit ashamed in one way. It would be his and Sari's birthday in another week, and he had intended to tell her that he wouldn't help her with the swimming lessons on that day. Now, of course, he wouldn't have to. But Sari was so grateful to him that he felt badly for ever having considered doing so.

On his birthday morning, Jed was awakened by Jared pouncing on his bed. "Happy birthday," he said, and rolled him over by the shoulder.

Jed's eyes weren't yet open. "Thanks," he said,

"but I'm not awake enough to appreciate it."

"Well, wake up," Jared told him. "You can't appreciate a day off if you're in bed all day and don't even know it. Come on, everybody is downstairs waiting for breakfast, and as one of the guests of honor, you're holding up the whole show."

Jed pulled on his bathrobe.

"Birthday boy first," said Jared. He held the door open and bowed low with a sweeping motion of his arm. Jed started down the stairs with Jared behind him. As he turned at the landing, he saw his grandfather sitting at the bottom of the stairs. Standing alongside him was Gretchen, hands on her hips, looking smug. His parents and Sari were there too.

"Happy birthday, Jed," called his grandfather.

"Thank you, Granddad."

No one else said anything. Gretchen just stood there with a funny look on her face.

It made Jed wonder. With his hand on the bannister, he paused on the last steps.

"Well, aren't you going to come the rest of the way down?" Gretchen demanded.

Jed said nothing. Filled with suspicion, he came stiffly down the last two steps. As he reached the bottom, Gretchen ducked behind Granddad's wheelchair, and then bounced back in front of him. "Happy birthday, Jed!" she cried, and into his middle, almost knocking him over, she shoved a smooth leather gun case.

Jed's heart leaped at the sight. He sank back

onto the steps. He could not believe what he held in his hands, yet the weight told him what was inside. Everyone was talking and laughing and clapping him on the back. "Open it," someone said.

Jed was weak with disbelief and excitement. He could hardly force his fingers to pull open the zipper. Finally it was undone. Within was the most beautiful rifle he had ever laid eyes on. His head was swimming as he pulled the long rifle from the case. It was a Remington automatic. The light glinted off the shiny new barrel and nearly blinded him. No words would come.

He looked up and saw Gretchen. She was beaming all over. So was Granddad. Then he saw Sari. It was her birthday, too, and she was empty-handed, yet smiling as if the rifle had been something special for her.

She read his thoughts. "Don't feel sorry for me, Jed. I am every bit as thrilled with knowing how to swim as you are with your rifle. I'm glad that you can be happy, too."

Dad wore a satisfied smile, and Mother was enjoying the entire affair.

Jed had trouble recovering from the unexpected surprise. "I just don't understand this," he said. "We never get birthday gifts, and there is less money now than ever with the cows milking so little. How could you get it?"

His grandfather answered. "There are some things you shouldn't worry about. It's good for a fellow to have a little encouragement now and then, even in hard times."

"Do you like it?" asked Gretchen.

"Like it!" said Jed. "Even in my wildest dreams, I never thought I would have a rifle for my birthday. I'm just going to sit and look at it all day."

His grandfather held out a box. "Here are some shells. It seemed this might be a good day to sight it in."

"This would be a good day for anything," said Jed. "I don't really know who to thank for it, so I'll thank all of you, everyone."

The family broke out with the birthday song, first for Jed, and then for Sari.

Later that day, Jed sat on the sandbank behind the barn. He had sighted the rifle at 50 and 100 yards, and it shot accurately. He ran his hand over one side of the rifle and back across the other. There wasn't a flaw in it. He sat in the warm sun and held the gun. It was strange, he thought, the way things worked out. Sometimes you wished so hard for something, and worked for it, too, and yet nothing went your way. And then, when you least expected it, your dreams came true. He wondered who was responsible for the unexpected surprise. His father certainly did not have the money, and yet all the family seemed to be aware of the happening.

It was afternoon when he walked back to the house, carrying his gun and picturing the way things would be when hunting season came in the fall. He stopped, pretending he had sighted a deer, raised the rifle, and aimed. He had heard about buck fever, though he didn't really understand what it was. Now he wondered if he would be stricken.

On the way home, he thought about Sari, too, and decided he would swim with her for a while if she was still in the water. She had been so excited about his rifle, completely unselfishly, and Jed was beginning to realize a new regard for her. Though she was physically weak, Sari did understand the hopes and needs of other people in a special way, and she really appreciated some things he just took for granted. Jed realized that she was not weak in every way.

Sari was sitting on the big oak limb that stretched out over the water.

"Hi," Jed said. "Do you want some company for a while?"

"Sure, even if I can't race you yet."

"From the way you're going, it won't be long," he said. He ran to the house, pulled on his swim trunks, and met Sari back at the lake.

"Perhaps I'll never swim as well as you do," she said, "but that isn't important. What matters is that I know how to do something well enough to like myself, and I am grateful to you for teaching me, Jed."

"That's OK."

"I guess you were pretty surprised about the rifle, weren't you?"

"I sure was."

"Are you going to show it to Emery?"

"Not until I happen to see him. I guess he'd think it wasn't as fancy as his, anyway, but I like it better than any rifle I've ever seen."

"I was sure you would. I knew how badly you wanted one.

"Do you feel any different," she asked then, "being a teenager, I mean?"

Jed shrugged. "I hadn't even thought about it. Do you?"

"I guess, a little." She sighed. "I wonder what things will happen while I'm 13." Her eyes looked far away.

Jed could see that there were still some things about Sari that he didn't understand. He only hoped that while he was 13 he would meet the Big One. At least he was equipped now, so if they did meet, he would be ready.

13

Hunting Season Again

THE OPENING OF SCHOOL in September meant a new venture for Jed, new classes, new teachers, and new friends. Especially in October, when the gun-safety course began, Jed's hunting ambition was kindled anew.

"Are you sure you don't want to take the course with me?" Jed asked Emery.

"Look," Emery said, "I've been shooting a gun and hunting for three years already. I know just about everything there is to know about a gun, and you said yourself that we still couldn't hunt alone until we're 14, even if we pass the course, so I just don't see any use in it."

"OK," said Jed, "suit yourself."

After the first session, Jed knew he'd learned more than he expected to learn during the whole course. The instructor explained the operation and advantage of every type of rifle and action and said that an open action was the only foolproof safety.

He pointed out that the decision to shoot would be Jed's alone, and he would have to accept the responsibility for the result. "It is absolutely essential that you make no mistakes," he continued. "You will be keyed up and alert for sounds and movements, and you must exercise strong control over your reactions."

Jed raised his hand. "What is buck fever?"

"Just what we're talking about. I have some people tell me that their knees start to shake, their eyes water, and they can feel their heart thud with every pump. Unless you can maintain strict control, your reflexes may cause you to shoot without you ever intending to."

On the school bus the next day, Jed asked Emery, "Do you know how many pounds of pressure it takes to release the total energy of a firearm?"

"I suppose at least 10 or 15."

"You're way off. Only four pounds. That's why a fellow has to be so careful how he handles a gun."

"Well," said Emery, "no dummy is going to shoot a gun unless he intends to, so what's the difference how much pressure it takes?"

"But we learned that the only foolproof safety is an open action."

Emery scoffed. "That guy doesn't know what he's talking about."

"Yes, he does," insisted Jed. He could hardly

wait for the next session, though he wished that Emery would go, too.

"Beware of hunting with untrained companions," the instructor began. "Select your hunting companion as you would choose someone for mountain climbing. Your life depends on your friend's skill and judgment."

Jed knew that he would never be able to hunt with Emery unless he could convince him to take the course. He decided to make one more try at persuading him.

"Did you know," he asked Emery, "that when you're hunting in a group, you have to decide on hunting zones so that your companions won't be in danger?"

"Quit pestering me," said Emery. "I know enough not to shoot anybody dressed in red, but I intend to get the game."

"Blaze orange is better than red."

Emery refused to be serious. "I look better in red. Orange is just not my color."

Jed quit talking. He knew that handling a gun was serious business, but the more he said to Emery, the sicker he felt.

He learned what to do if he should become lost in the woods, or if someone was hurt. Many of these were commonsense items, some of which he had learned from his father long ago.

On the firing range, he came out with a perfect score, but he worried through the week until the day of the written test. He knew what Emery would have to say if he didn't pass.

After the test, Jed came home and burst through the door, waving his Hunter Safety Badge and Certificate. "I made it!" he called. He felt 100 percent qualified as a hunter.

"I knew you would," said Sari.

"Well, you were a lot more sure than I was, but I only missed two questions."

"Now all you have to do is find a deer," said Gretchen.

Mother looked up from her sewing. "And I hope he does. We have only a few packages of meat left in the freezer."

"We could butcher a cow, couldn't we?" Jed asked.

"Not this year," said his father. "Our only income is from milk, and we have to keep every cow."

"Couldn't we cut some more logs?"

"We could," said his father, "but the mill isn't paying until after the first of February. That really puts a crimp in things."

Jed was troubled. He went to his grandfather's room. "I'd always felt we could count on the woods for extra income," he said. "That's one reason I love this place. I thought everything would be all right here, and now that isn't true either."

"That's not the fault of the woods," said Granddad. "The trees are still there, and will be until you're ready to cut them, but a deer is the product of the woods, too. If you can supply the family with meat, that's as good as money."

His grandfather was right. "I hadn't pictured it quite that way."

Jed lay back on the bed and thought about the hunting season ahead. Now there was even greater reason to get a deer, and the Big One in particular. That being the case, he'd better start doing something about it.

Every day after school, Jed went into the woods looking for buck rubs, deer beds, or other signs that would indicate the presence of deer. He intended to hunt where he found the most signs.

The air was becoming brisk and cold, but the days were bright. The ground was covered with a heavy mat of fallen leaves which crackled underfoot, and it was a pleasure being in the woods. Checking a different place each afternoon, Jed always returned in 45 minutes or an hour, leaving plenty of time to do his chores before dark.

The ground began to freeze, and it became more difficult to locate tracks. A week before deer season opened, the wind howled from the north. Jed watched the surface water of the small lake as it was whipped along by the wind and carried to the far end, one sweep after another. The sky turned gray, and the water was dark and cold. Jed shuddered. He liked to swim and skate, but the icy water on the move sent an uncertain quiver clear through him.

By morning the wind had quieted and the lake was frozen over. On the following nights, the temperature dipped to unusual lows, and Jed knew that neither the ground nor the lake would be thawed again until spring.

The deer season was to open on Saturday morning. On Friday, Dad went into town for boots and other equipment for Jed. "Your mother is going with me," he said. "We may be late getting home. Be sure to do the chores on time."

"Don't worry," said Jed. "I'll see to it that things get started."

The day had been cold and sunny, but when they were riding home from school, the sky had turned dark and it soon began to snow heavily.

Jed was thoroughly excited. "This means good tracking in the morning," he said to Emery. "I can hardly wait. Did your dad get that new rifle he was talking about?"

"No, he didn't. He got too busy to do anything about it. He'll be hunting with the same gun he always used. Are you going out early?"

"You bet we are." He called good-bye as Emery left the bus. "Good luck," he said.

"Thanks. Drive by tomorrow night and see my buck hanging in the yard."

Jed moved to sit with Sari. "As soon as we get home," he said, "I'm going out for a half hour to check for tracks south of the lake. I have to be back early to help Jared start the chores."

116

"All right," said Sari. "Mother asked me to start the supper and help Gretchen with her reading."

At home, Jed peeked in his grandfather's room. He was napping. Jed changed his clothes and started down the east side of the lake toward the south end. The snow was still falling heavily, but no wind stirred. Jed searched the ground for tracks, but sighted none.

Climbing up the high ridge, he spotted tracks crossing the logging road. Excitement flared within him. He knew they had been made only minutes before, as the snow would have covered them almost immediately. It was still in the woods as he ran along following the tracks. They were large, and the animal did not seem to be in any particular hurry. As Jed realized that the tracks were leading to the Christmas tree swamp, his steps grew faster. He remembered a heavy snow last year just before he had seen the Big One in the swamp.

The tracks went on, veering now and then in an off direction, but then coming back on course toward the swamp.

Jed was almost out of breath. Coming over the last rise, he felt certain that the deer was in the swamp, and that it was the Big One. Pursuing it further would be the wrong thing to do. If the deer had entered the swamp, Jed's coming would surely scare him out.

He stopped. He suddenly realized he had been in

117

pursuit without actually thinking about what he was doing. He was a long way from the lake and a long way from home. He felt in his pockets. All he had for equipment were matches. It was nearly dark. He had lost all track of time, and he had promised to have the chores started early.

Jed looked around him. The deer tracks, as well as his own, were completely covered. Never had he felt so alone. He knew where he was, but in the heavy snowfall the woods seemed entirely strange. The silence was as thick as the snow. A chill crept through his veins as he turned and started for home.

14

Lost

JED HURRIED OVER THE RIDGE, intending to re-
trace his path, yet realizing that under the present
conditions he could easily become confused.

At home, Sari was busy with the supper, and in
between peeling potatoes and putting a cake in the
oven, she helped Gretchen with her words. Jared
had gone outdoors to start the chores.

Gretchen sat by the window. "Turn the light on,
Sari. It's getting dark."

Sari switched on the light. "It *is* getting dark."
She ran to the window and peered out toward the
lake, then glanced at the clock. "I can hardly see
anything, and Jed has been gone over an hour and
a half. I think he's lost."

Gretchen saw the fear in Sari's eyes. "It looks
awful out there. Can you find him?"

"Gretchen, will you promise me that you'll stay

in the house and not go outside, no matter what happens?"

"I promise."

"Then I'm going to look for Jed. I'll go to the end of the lake and call. I can't go into the woods, but it is quiet and he should be able to hear a long ways. If Mother and Dad come home or if Jared comes in, tell them where I am. I'm sure Granddad is still sleeping, but you can go in and wake him up if you feel afraid or anything."

Sari glanced at the road as she left the house. The snow was already several inches deep, and no traffic had passed for some time. She waved to Gretchen in the window, and trudged across the frozen lake.

In the meantime, Jed had been traveling toward home at a fast and steady pace. At any minute he expected to reach the landing where he and his father had logged. Though he knew he should be in familiar surroundings, everything looked strange. Concern rose in his mind with every step.

Tiring, he stopped to lean against a broken tree. He was angry with himself for forgetting time and his chores, but he was frightened, too. Then he remembered his instructor's words: "The only thing to be afraid of in the woods is losing your head."

He tried desperately to organize his thinking. He knew for certain that he had been at the Christmas tree swamp. That was definite, and he thought he had followed a straight course on the way back. But there was no sun to guide him by, and his father had told him that he could walk in circles on such a day and not even know it.

Jed felt in his pockets again. He squeezed his eyes to shut out the despair. How could he spend the night in the woods without equipment? To make matters worse, it was dark already.

Again he tried to figure out his position. The area was high, and that gave him a spark of hope. The landing had to be somewhere close. He remembered hearing traffic on the road and the school bus in their driveway when he had been high in the woods before. He stopped and listened, motionless, straining his ears for any sound. There was nothing. The silence was terrifying.

Filled with panic, he fled to the left, thinking he had to be going north. Surely he would come to the lake. Then, somewhere in the distance, he heard a muffled scream. Jed stopped, his heart pounding.

He heard it again. It seemed to be coming from behind him. It was against his judgment—that would be south—and there was nothing there. He yelled back as loud as he could, "Hello!"

The yell came again. It *was* behind him. He whirled and ran 30 feet. "Hello!" he called. The scream came again. Someone must be hunting for him. He raced another 30 feet, right to the landing he knew so well. In his fright, he had been going in the wrong direction earlier. He felt ashamed.

He heard the scream again, this time more clearly. "Help, help!"

Someone else was in trouble. He was sure the voice came from near the lake. "I'm coming!" yelled Jed. He raced frantically, stumbling over broken branches and treetops in the thickening darkness. At the edge of the ridge, he yelled again, "Where are you?"

"Jed, help me!" The voice came from below. It was Sari!

Jed's heart leaped in his chest. Surely she had come to find him. Then he heard the cracking of ice and splashing of water. She had broken through! "Hang on, Sari! I'm coming!"

Jed slid, fell, and smashed into trees as he plunged down the steep embankment. The snow had stopped, and he could see a dark figure in the lake. He knew it was the work of otters—the lake had been safe.

"Don't try to climb out!" he called. The ice was not thick enough to support her weight. "Hang onto the edge and keep kicking."

Jed found a long sturdy branch. He grabbed it and ran onto the ice.

"You'll go through!" Sari called.

Jed lay down and slid on his stomach, pushing the pole ahead. He inched nearer, and the pole slid across. "Grab hold!" he yelled. "And climb out toward me."

He felt her grasp the pole. She was crying. "I

"Grab hold and climb out toward me."

can't make it, Jed. My legs won't move anymore."

"Don't let go!" He crept on his stomach, keeping his weight on the pole. Stretching for every inch, he grasped her firmly by the wrist. "Lie down over the pole."

She tried to help. Jed pulled with every ounce of strength in his body. He raised her over the pole, and crawled backward, skidding her away from the hole.

"Don't leave me," she pleaded.

"I'm going to get you home." Jed saw that there was no way she could walk. She was almost paralyzed from the icy water. He took off his jacket and wrapped it around her.

Dashing to an evergreen at the lake's edge, he grabbed a high branch and jumped, coming down with his full weight. It snapped off. He rolled Sari onto the branch. "Hang on," he said.

The snow was deep, and Jed's legs were exhausted, but he stumbled on because he knew Sari would be frozen before long.

Nearing home, he heard his father calling. He was coming toward them. "Sari! Sari!"

"Over here!" yelled Jed. "I've got her!"

His father ran toward them.

"She went through the ice, Dad. She's almost frozen."

Sari's winter clothing was soaked and heavy, but Dad took her in his arms and ran up the hill to the house.

"Get her clothes off!" Dad said. While Mother quickly pulled off Sari's icy garments, Jed ran to the closest room, his grandfather's, and pulled the blankets from the bed. They wrapped them tightly around Sari. She was shaking violently. Jed warmed another blanket and they put it next to her skin.

She tried to speak. "Jed didn't come back," she said. "I thought he was lost."

"Sari, please," he said. "Don't try to talk. Just rest."

"John," Mother whispered. "We'd better call the doctor. I think that her lungs are filling."

Jed looked into Sari's eyes. They were stunned and distant. Fear surged in his heart. It was all his fault because he had forgotten his responsibilities.

His mother came back from the phone. "The doctor says we must get her to the hospital in the city where they have the facilities she needs. No one can get through the roads, but he's sending the plow and ambulance out. It will be at least an hour until they get here. In the meantime, we're to keep her warm and calm."

Sari heard, and there was terror in her eyes. "Mama, don't let them take me away," she pleaded.

Her mother tried to reassure her. "Sari, you must go to the hospital. We don't have an oxygen tent and other things that are going to be needed for you."

"Then come with me, and stay." Sari's breathing was labored, and she was near hysteria.

"Go, Mother," Jed said. "I'll take care of the house."

Mother's eyes filled with tears. "I wish I could stay with her every instant, but we just spent our last money in town. There isn't even a cent left for the hospital, let alone any money to rent a room for me to stay nearby. You know there isn't room for me to stay at Uncle George's house, and I'm not sure they'd let me stay with Sari at the hospital."

Jed looked at Sari again. He knew she would die if they sent her away alone.

15

Another Rifle

ALL THE LOVE Jed had denied his sister for their 13 years swelled within him. He put his arms around her. "Sari," he whispered, "Mother will go with you. I promise."

Jed placed his hand on his father's shoulder. "I'll be back before the plow and ambulance come."

Quickly he ran to his room for his rifle. He buttoned his jacket around him. In the garage he found the snowshoes. Strapping them on, he lit out at a running pace for the Daager house.

Getting the Big One would have to wait. He had to do what he could to save Sari.

Though the shoes were awkward and he was already exhausted, he drove himself on. The Daagers had to be home, unless they had left right after school before the snow piled up. He saw a light in the window. Jed quickened his stride. He pulled his feet out of the snowshoes, ran up the steps, and hammered on the door. It seemed an eternity until it opened.

"Mr. Daager," he said, "my sister is terribly sick, and I need some money right away. Could you use this rifle?" He held it forward.

"That yours?"

"Yes, the one I got for my birthday. Emery has seen it."

Mr. Daager nodded. "I'll give you $75.00 cash."

"That's good enough."

Mr. Daager counted it out—50, 60, 70, and 75.

Jed handed him the rifle and the box of shells from his pocket. "Thanks, Mr. Daager," he said.

Emery stood in the background. Jed's eyes met his; but for once, Emery had nothing to say.

Jed knelt to strap the snowshoes on once more, and started for home. Behind him, he saw a flashing blue light, and behind that, a red one. The plow and ambulance were coming for Sari. Jed hurried faster, but his knees buckled and he fell in the snow.

Raising himself, he staggered to the edge of the road and waited for the plow, signaling for the driver to stop. "I'm Jed Craig," he said. "Could I have a ride with you?"

"Climb in. You look pretty tuckered out. I understand your sister's sick."

"She is."

"We'll get her to the hospital. It's a good thing I

was in the shop when the doctor called. I was about ready to leave on the regular patrol."

At the house, Jed threw the snowshoes out of the cab and then jumped out and ran inside.

Sari's every breath made a hideous drawing sound. Her face was a strange bluish color.

Jed pressed the money into his mother's hand. "Go," he said, "and take care of Sari. We'll be praying."

Mother squeezed his hand. Through the tears she could say nothing, but her eyes told him all that was in her heart. She bent to kiss Gretchen.

The ambulance attendants were strapping Sari to the stretcher. They put an oxygen mask over her nose and mouth.

Jed bent over her. "Mother is going with you," he said, and he thought she understood.

He watched from the window as the flashing red light disappeared into the darkness.

His grandfather was at the kitchen doorway. "I made some sandwiches," he said. "Come and eat."

The mention of food made Jed feel sick. His arms and legs went limp. His father helped him to his grandfather's room. Jed lay on the bed, his eyes closed, and his hands locked behind his head. He whispered a simple prayer that all would be well with Sari. Then, exhausted, he dropped off to sleep.

Sometime later, he was awakened by the sound of the door opening. Hearing no footsteps, his eyes opened instinctively. It was his grandfather, sitting in his wheelchair beside the bed. Across his lap lay a cotton gun case, faded and worn.

Jed watched in silence as his grandfather untied each securing knot and carefully took a rifle from the case.

Jed had never seen the gun.

"She's an old timer, Jed." His grandfather's wrinkled fingers stroked down to the muzzle in remembrance. "She got me my first buck there along the North Fork of the Flambeau River when I was about your age. She belonged to your great-granddad."

He turned the old rifle over and worked the lever action. Satisfied, he raised it to position, pulled the butt snug against his shoulder, and aimed toward the window.

Lowering it, his eyes met Jed's. They were filled with an excitement that Jed had not noticed before. "And if you're a good shot," he said, "it can get one for you, too."

Jed unlocked his hands and sat up on the edge of the bed facing his grandfather. The gun was offered with outstretched hands, and Jed reached to accept it. "It can use a lot of shining on the outside," his grandfather said. "It's seen a few good clubs and nicks, but I've kept it clean, and I've got plenty of ammunition. It's pretty hard to buy shells for a rifle like this anymore."

Jed opened the action. It was every bit as clean as the new rifle he'd just sold.

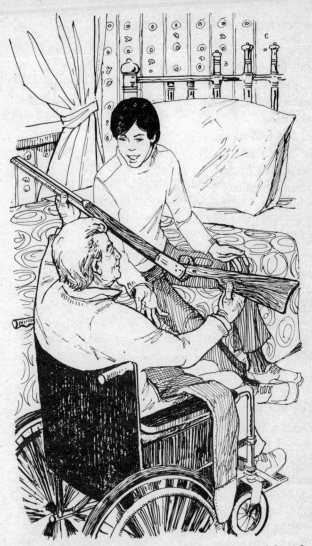

Granddad offered the gun with outstretched hands, and Jed reached to accept it.

"You'd have to save the empties and reload them."

Jed raised the rifle to his shoulder and aimed outside the window at a branch of the bare maple tree which was hardly visible even with the yard light still on.

"It's the long barrel that makes her heavy," said his grandfather, "but you're strong—you can handle her. She takes ten shells in the magazine. There's no worry about running short. 'Course, she's not as fast as an automatic, but she's as fast as the fellow that uses it."

Jed looked at his grandfather questioningly.

"I've seen you shoot 'round here, Jed. You're fast enough to get any whitetail in these parts."

Jed lowered his eyes, but he appreciated the expressed confidence. He turned the rifle over several times. "Where did Great-granddad get this rifle?" he asked.

"It's an 1894 Winchester, made only 30 years after the Civil War. My dad traded a .303 Savage for it when I was a little fellow. The Savage shot too far, and he was afraid it would hurt someone. He was a peaceable man, and only wanted a gun he could depend on for the family's supply of meat. The trapper he traded with needed a gun for protection."

Jed's interest was aroused. He pictured a grown young man, looking somewhat like himself, standing before a small log cabin and trading guns with a rugged frontiersman. Behind him, near the partly opened door, he saw a small boy cautiously eyeing the proceedings. That would be Granddad, later to carry the rifle on his first hunt.

Jed leaned forward. "I'll be ready in the morning, Granddad. Where do you keep the shells?"

16

Hopes

JED SLEPT LITTLE that night. The events of the previous day would not leave his mind. Even when he did drop off to sleep, he was troubled by strange and confusing dreams. Once he awoke in a cold sweat, dreaming that Sari had slipped from his grasp and had disappeared beneath the dark, icy water. It was a long and fitful night, and Jed was glad when his father called him to get up early in the morning.

He pulled on his clothes and shoes and ran downstairs. "Did you have a phone call in the night, Dad?"

"Yes," said his father. "Your mother said Sari is holding her own."

"I pray she is. Last night I was afraid for her life."

"So was I." Dad's voice lowered. "That was a real sacrifice you made, Jed."

Jed looked at his father. "It was what had to be done."

"I understand."

"Granddad gave me his father's rifle."

His father nodded. "We'd better get started."

Jed told his father about the big tracks leading to the swamp.

"In that case," Dad said, "we'd better try there first. I'll circle and come in toward the swamp from the south. You take your regular route."

"All right," said Jed. "I'll choose a stand to the west of the swamp."

"It will take me a little longer to reach my position," said his father. "Fifteen minutes should give me enough of a head start. When you get to your stand, wait an hour and give him a chance to come out on his own account. If I don't see or hear anything in that time, I'll start into the swamp slightly to the south. Be on guard, and good luck."

Jed waited 15 minutes after his father had left. Then he put on two extra shirts, his red wool jacket, and blaze orange cap.

His grandfather wheeled himself out from his room. "It's going to be good tracking out there. It isn't often you get it that good the first day of deer season. You have enough shells?"

"Fifteen. If I don't get one with that many, I guess there's no hope anyway,"

"Good luck, Jed."

"Thanks, Granddad—for everything."

Jed started toward the lake. Reaching the shoreline, he stopped and loaded the gun—ten shells—all it would hold. He opened the action to put one shell in the chamber and clicked the hammer in the safety position.

The sky in the east showed the first inklings of dawn as he came to the south end of the lake and climbed the steep embankment. Reaching the top, he looked down to the lake where last night's life-or-death struggle had taken place. Though it was still too dark to see, it was unbelievable that everything could be so peaceful here now. He was still uneasy, and he told himself that he probably would not be in the woods at all if it wasn't that his family needed meat. Perhaps, he thought, when Sari had regained her health, he could rest easy.

The snap of a twig sounded behind him. Jed remained motionless. Only his eyes moved stealthily from one side to the other. Should it be a deer, any quick movement would send it tearing from sight.

He heard another snap, more to the right. Though it was becoming daylight, Jed was not certain that he would yet be able to see the sights of the rifle. Very slowly he turned.

The snap sounded again. It was a gray squirrel, scampering on a pile of brush. Jed was amused at himself for having become so tense.

Then he became angry. In the minutes he had thought a deer was at hand, he had forgotten all about Sari lying desperately ill in the hospital. What would she think of him? He wanted to run for home, yet he knew Dad was depending on him. He rubbed his forehead, trying to clear his thinking. What *would* Sari think? he asked again.

Then he knew. When he had been given the rifle for his birthday, she was more excited than if it had been for her. If he wasn't successful on the hunt, or hadn't even gone, she would blame herself because he had sold the rifle in her behalf. But if he could bring in a deer, she would be overjoyed.

He looked at the rifle. He thought of his father counting on him, and Granddad's excitement. Courage and determination which had generated from his family, even ages back, rose and flowed within him. His was that kind of a family, and Jed was humbly proud to be a part of it.

"Get well, Sari," he said aloud. "I'm going to bring you the best and biggest venison roast you ever saw, and I've got our great-granddad's rifle here to do it."

17

The Big One

IT WAS ALMOST LIGHT, and Jed hurried toward the swamp. There were no tracks anywhere. He surveyed in all directions, yet kept his mind on his prime objective. He slowed down as he was coming over the rise, moving cautiously and holding onto small trees so that he would not slip.

The swamp stretched in full view. Jed's eyes searched the edge. No tracks were visible. Either the Big One was still in the swamp or had simply passed through last night. But, somehow, Jed felt that the swamp was the Big One's home.

He chose a stand from which he could cover the most territory, near a big oak with a large knotty growth about four feet from the ground. He tried resting his arm against the knot. It fit well. He would be able to steady himself if the time came to shoot.

Half an hour passed. His father was waiting, too. That meant he had seen no tracks leaving in his direction.

Patiently he waited. The sun was rising over the hill to the east. Soon it would be difficult to see. Jed hoped his father would come before then.

Another half hour passed. He trained his eyes on the swamp and attuned his ears for the slightest sound, but there was no movement, and silence hung low.

Suddenly a swishing noise caught Jed's ear. It came from the swamp. He moved his thumb to the hammer and tightened his grip on the rifle. From the inner swamp came another stirring. An evergreen shed its covering of snow. The snow slid from a nearer tree. It was either a deer or his father coming through the swamp.

Jed peered intensely. Between two evergreens, slightly to the north, he spied the front shoulders of a huge white-tailed deer. Cautiously he raised the rifle and waited for the deer to come into the open. His heart thudded heavily against his ribs as he leaned against the knot on the tree.

A huge rack of horns was protruding from behind a tree. Jed pulled the hammer back, releasing the safety. The animal moved forward until its front half was in full view. It was the Big One, magnificent against the background of white, the most beautiful white-tailed buck Jed had ever laid eyes on.

It was in his sights, but suddenly his father's words echoed in his ears, "Even when you know they're mature, you have to think a long time." Jed knew it was needed.

In the instant he had taken to think, the Big One tensed, sensing trouble. He bolted forward with a mighty leap. Jed caught him again in the sights at the crest of the rise and squeezed the trigger. The deer fell with a heave, then rose to his feet and lunged over the hill.

Jed pumped another shell into the chamber, but the Big One had disappeared. He ran after him, carrying the rifle in both hands. His legs felt weak and shaky.

Reaching the spot where the buck had dropped, he saw that blood was spilled in the snow. He ran up the hill, following the trail. Just over the crest lay the Big One. Jed slid to a stop. He breathed a sigh of relief as he propped the gun against a tree.

His father appeared over the rise. "Good shooting, Son."

Jed gazed at the downed animal. "He didn't really have a chance."

"Jed, all I could see were the back quarters, but I saw him lunge before I heard the shot. Do you know how easy it is to miss a shot like that?" He knelt beside Jed. "I know how you feel. Hunting an animal isn't all glory, but when it's needed, it has to be."

"When I first thought about hunting, I sure had

a different idea," admitted Jed.

"Is that why you waited?"

Jed nodded.

Together they dressed out the animal, tied a rope to its horns, and began the long pull out of the woods. It was near noon when they reached the ridge.

Jed kicked the snow off a stump and sat down. "Let's take a rest before we start across the lake."

"That's hard work," Dad said, sitting down beside him. He took a sandwich from his pocket. "My stomach tells me it's time for lunch."

Jed ate a sandwich too. They started down the steep hillside, and onto the lake. Halfway across, they saw Jared running toward them. "Mother just called. Sari is out of danger," he hollered as he neared them.

The words they were both waiting to hear.

They saw Granddad and Gretchen smiling at the window.

When Jared reached them, he grabbed Jed by the shoulders. "Did *you* get it?"

"You bet he did!" His father grinned broadly. "It's the Big One. Jed did some mighty fine shooting, too."

"Good for you, Jed! I knew you could do it." Jared clapped him on the back.

Jared remembered. "One more thing," he said. "Mother saw Emery just before she called—at the hospital. He shot himself in the hand going out to

142

the woods. He'll be all right, as long as no infection sets in."

Jed was astounded. Poor Emery. Would he ever learn?

"He had a message for you. He's going to take the safety course next year."

Jed felt like he could hardly take any more good news. He looked again at the window where his grandfather and sister waited. He raised the head of the Big One with one hand, and taking the aged rifle in the other, he thrust it several times at arm's length in the air, proclaiming triumph. He smiled widely, his dark eyes shining.

His grandfather understood. He returned a silent cheer from the window, and Gretchen blew kisses.

"Come on," said Jed. "Let's get home."